D1040934

the

d e

AN IMPRINT OF DISNEY BOOK GROUP

For my parents and my girls

Text copyright © 2008 by Kathryn Williams
All rights reserved. Published by Hyperion Books for Children, an imprint of
Disney Book Group. No part of this book may be reproduced or transmitted in
any form or by any means, electronic or mechanical, including photocopying,
recording, or by any information storage and retrieval system, without
written permission from the publisher. For information address
Hyperion Books for Children,
114 Fifth Avenue, New York, New York 10011-5690.

Printed in the United States of America
First Edition
1 3 5 7 9 10 8 6 4 2
Library of Congress Cataloging-in-Publication Data on file.
ISBN 978-1-4231-0045-4
Reinforced binding
Designed by Roberta Pressel
Visit www.hyperionteens.com

prologue

There are a number of scenarios a girl is genetically compelled to spend hour after unproductive hour of her young adult life imagining: her first kiss, her second kiss, the long-awaited freedom of a driver's license, her senior year of high school . . . to name a few. Now, imagine if—after all that imagining—everything you had planned on was turned upside down and inside out. Then you would be imagining my life.

The bomb was dropped in May. "The bomb" being the news that my dad had been offered a "once-in-a-lifetime" (unfortunately, *my* lifetime) opportunity to head up the new American Studies department at Queen Anne's College . . . in Beaufort . . . Alabama.

Beaufort is where my father grew up, a mere *one thousand* miles from where I grew up, in Connecticut. I had known, of course, that he was looking to move to a new school, but down South? And when I had only one year left of high school? I was pretty sure that in some circles that qualified as child abuse.

After the announcement, World War III erupted at our house, and the worst part was that my parents presented a united front. I'd been sure my mother would be my most important ally in the anti-Beaufort campaign. She's a photographer, and often commuted to Manhattan. I couldn't imagine her creativity flourishing in a place where I was convinced neon signage was considered "high art."

But apparently, the old man had gotten to her first.

That didn't stop me from trying.

I appealed to the New Yorker in her: "Where will we get decent bagels? And lox? And pizza?" I asked. "These are people who consider fried pork rinds a delicacy."

"Annie, please don't give me a headache," my mother responded, her hands moving dramatically to her temples. "We're all in this together."

I played on her sympathy: "Who will I hang out with?"

"You'll make friends and have an amazing senior year," she assured me as she bubble-wrapped knickknacks.

"Right. I'm sure I'll fit in perfectly with the Southern belles," I volleyed back. "We're Connecticut people, Mom. I play sports; they cheer for them. I go to Widespread concerts; they go to tractor pulls."

"You can hang out with your cousins, then," was her reply.

"Charlotte and Virginia?" I practically snorted in disbelief. My cousins were blond-haired, blue-eyed replicas of each other, who distinguished themselves only by their respective hobbies: horseback riding and cheerleading.

"They're in like, ninth grade! Besides, I haven't seen them since I was ten, and they were already terrible then. They made me play *Gone with the Wind* with their Barbies!" I spat out the last sentence as if my cousins had tried to talk me into a friendly game of Light Little Kittens on Fire.

My mother ignored me.

So I pulled out the big guns. "I'm trying to get into Brown! How is my transcript going to look with a senior year at Podunk High?" It was a legitimate concern, I felt. We were talking Ivy League, here. Unless Brown had some sort of redneck quota to fill, I was afraid a diploma issued in Alabama might not exactly be an asset in the college admissions process.

"Beaufort Country Day is one of the best schools in the South," my mother replied. "It did produce your father."

I was at a loss. Brown had been my trump card. I'd dreamed of going there essentially since I came out of the womb. My father got his PhD there, and while he never explicitly encouraged me to go, he always got a stupid grin on his face when I wore the ratty, old Brown University sweatshirt he'd given me. When I told him I'd decided to apply early decision, he'd taken us out for an impromptu dinner in the city (so very *not* my dad).

Now Brown wasn't just my first choice, it was also my ticket out of Dixie. My persuasive powers had failed me. I had lost the war. I had no idea why two cultured, liberal, supposedly intelligent people would voluntarily move to the home of segregation, Forrest Gump, and—worst of all—my grandmother.

But we were going.

To Beaufort.

Alabama.

ONE

A lady doesn't sweat, she glistens.

The overwhelming scent of magnolia wafted through my bedroom on a humid breeze. If I leaned out the window, I could almost touch the tree's glossy, dark green leaves. When the woman from the real estate company gave us a tour of the house, my mother had optimistically called the tree "charming," but at the moment, in the August heat, the aroma was utterly noxious.

All morning I had been helping my parents unpack the kitchen, until, more out of an urge to get away from them than any irresistible desire to settle into our new home, I had firmly announced I was ready to tackle my room. Sitting amid the brown cardboard boxes stacked like building blocks, I considered how soul crushing it was to see all of my earthly belongings packed up and labeled "Annie's Things." It was the end of the world as I knew it, and all I had to console myself were relics of my past life—pictures and ticket stubs, old notes, and a "care package" Jamie, my best friend, had sent with me, with the insistence that it should be opened only when I *really, really* needed it. I figured now was as good a time as any and fished the shoe box from its bed of packing peanuts.

A knock at the door startled me. When I didn't answer immediately, it creaked open to reveal my mother. The stifling heat was bothering her, too, I could tell. Her hair was pulled back in a loose bun, and sweat stains had appeared under the arms of her orange T-shirt. With the air-conditioning on the fritz, we'd had to use knives to pry open the windows, most of which were painted shut, to avoid suffocation. Not that this was much help with the humidity, through which we could have breast-stroked. And the cherry on top: we were evidently below the "gnat line," where there were more bugs than humans.

"Are you still moping?" my mom asked from the doorway.

"I prefer 'mourning,'" I answered, running my hand over the lid of the shoe box, which Jamie had decoupaged with photos and magazine clippings. "And yes."

Crossing the room to plant herself on my quilted bedspread (entirely too hot, I'd already realized, for the Seventh Circle of Hell in which we now lived), my mom sighed. I could feel her watching me, but I refused to return her gaze.

"Haven't you ever wished you could have a fresh start?" she pleaded. "This is a chance to reinvent yourself!"

"I've spent seventeen years inventing myself," I said, finally looking up from my new itchy, ugly carpet. "Why would I want to start all over again?" Wiping at the beads of sweat collecting on my upper lip, I stared at her and fought the building pressure of tears. An all-too-familiar feeling these days.

She didn't have an answer. And, all joking aside, I didn't want a fresh start. I wanted Connecticut and Deerwood Academy and Jamie. A framed picture of us stared up at me from her package. It was from Halloween, the year we'd dressed as ketchup and mustard. Our skinny legs stuck out from painted foam-board costumes as we grinned at the camera. Jamie was making the peace sign, her middle and forefinger spread into a triumphant V.

Under different circumstances, the photo would have made me smile. Now it made me feel entirely lost. Lost and adrift. Which, if you were to ask Jamie, were two feelings I valiantly opposed on a general basis. I was *not* a girl who liked change. I had lived in the same house for thirteen years, from the age of four. I'd had the same best friend since third grade and the same poster above my bed since roughly the same era. I even hated getting a haircut. Adaptation was not on my agenda.

"Well," my mother sighed again as she stood to leave, "I just wanted to remind you that we have dinner at the country club with your grandparents at six."

I stifled a groan. I hadn't seen my grandparents since I was ten, when Camp Chinakwa and field hockey clinics started to replace my annual summer visit to Gram and Pawpaw MacRae's. But I still vividly remembered my days at Belmont, the creaky, old plantation house where my father was raised. The house was magical; unfortunately, the company was not. Gram was always too busy to play (besides the fact I'd never been convinced she actually *liked* children), which left me with the twin terrors, Virginia and Charlotte, or Roberta, Gram's housekeeper, who didn't talk much but let me snap green beans on Belmont's sagging front porch.

It wasn't all bad. I remembered nights of spotlight tag and chasing lightning bugs around mammoth magnolias. And the sour, metallic smell the bugs gave off if you kept them in a jar too long or forgot to poke airholes. One summer I'd convinced Virginia and Charlotte that the house was haunted by the ghosts of slaves. Of course they'd told their mother, Aunt Nonny, who'd chased me around the yard with a switch from the weeping willow, only causing me to laugh harder.

Yet despite those moments, I always came away from my visits at Belmont with the sinking feeling that there was an essential disconnect between who I was and who Gram thought I should be. The older I'd gotten, the more interest she had taken in me, but it was interest I could have done without. One summer—my last at Belmont coincidentally—Gram had driven me to Beaufort's fanciest department store and told me I could pick out any dress I wanted. After staring at the rows and rows of pink smocking and lavender ruffles, I had opted instead for a pair of jean overalls because Jamie owned ones just like them. Gram had gotten me a dress—with ruffles—anyway.

Since that fateful summer, my relationship with my grandparents had been reduced to biannual monetary installments at Christmas and birthdays. Without fail, twice a year, I could expect a big, fat check, along with a demitasse spoon on my birthday. (My mother had to explain to me that the tiny silver spoons weren't for babies, but for fancy tea. I didn't think I'd ever use them, but as long as they were accompanied by that check, I'd take them.) I could also count on the mandatory thank-you notes my father made me write—the only time I ever used the monogrammed stationery Gram had given me when I turned thirteen.

"And you might want to wear a dress," my mother said now, flooding me with the same panicky feeling I'd experienced seven years ago in the department store.

"No way," I insisted. "That's ridiculous. I'm not dressing up for Gram and a bunch of her snobby old friends at 'the Club'!"

Turning, her hands on her hips, my mom assumed

her irritated look. "I'm not asking you to get dressed up, Annie. Why don't you just wear that green sundress? The one with the big flowers."

I glanced around the bare, white room, at all the boxes still to be unpacked and the skeletal hangers in the empty closet. "Maybe. If I can find it," I granted, which roughly translated into "fat chance."

"Thank you," she said before disappearing down the hall. Two seconds later she poked her head back in the room. "Annie," she said softly this time, "I really hope you can try to be happy here."

I looked at her but didn't answer. I had really *hoped* they'd wait until after I'd graduated to move. But, as I was quickly learning, you don't always get what you want.

TWO

*A lady always sends
a thank-you note.*

Above the noise of a thousand sprinklers, I could hear
the click of my mother's heels on the brick portico. I
followed my parents past tennis courts and an emerald-
green golf course, toward the stately, white-columned
establishment formally called the Beaufort Country Club
but known to my grandparents simply as, "the Club."

Entering the dark grill room, we were greeted by a
welcome blast of icy air-conditioning. I shivered at the
contrast in temperature and nearly stumbled down the
stairs as my eyes adjusted to the dim lighting. The room
was paneled in oak and lined with plaid banquettes and
heavy, wooden tables. Three middle-aged men in pastel golf shirts and khakis sat puffing cigars in front of a
fireplace at the far end of the long room. Their sudden
eruption into loud guffaws made me more than slightly
uncomfortable.

My grandparents were sitting at a large corner table,
under a stuffed deer head. As we crossed the room, I
could feel its sad, little Bambi eyes watching me. Paired
with the grave stares of the bearded, gray men whose

portraits hung on the walls, it gave me the creepy feeling that I was in one of those haunted houses where the eyes of paintings follow you.

Gram and Pawpaw—flanked by my father's sister Nonny, her husband, Tripp, the twins, and their comparably tolerable older brother, Richard—held court at opposite ends of the table. Catching Richard's bored eye, I nodded. It was too bad he'd be back at college soon. He seemed a potential sympathizer.

"Gordon, dear! We were just wondering if we were going to have to order without you." Gram stood from the table, cocked her head to the side with a smile, and held her arms out in front of her for a hug and brisk peck on the cheek from her son. She wore a pale pink linen suit with pink pumps and matching pearl brooch and earrings. A little more gray was peeking through her bottle-blond hair, and a few more wrinkles lined her powdered face, but Gram's posture was still stick straight and her appearance immaculate.

Without a doubt, this was the same woman who had made me eat my peas before shuffling us out to the yard so she and her bridge club "might have some peace and quiet." Not exactly the warm and fuzzy grandma with arts-and-crafts projects and a plate of freshly baked cookies waiting. Until I'd met Jamie's "Nana," a stout woman with purple-tinged hair who smelled like gingerbread, I had assumed those grandmothers only existed on television and in greeting cards.

"Hi, Mother," my father said dutifully. "Sorry, we were unpacking and lost track of time." He bent down to give Gram her kiss.

"That's all right, dear. I'm just thrilled to have you back. Judith, you look well." With one barely perceptible swoop of the eyes, Gram looked my mother—wearing a sleeveless, chocolate-colored wrap dress—up and down. "Brown is the new black, I see?"

"Hi, Mary," my mother responded evenly, declining to take the bait. "Good to see you."

And then, it was my turn.

"Ann Gordon," Gram cooed, taking my hands.

Five minutes, and already I was searching for the emergency exits. Ann Gordon. I was "Annie" to everyone but my grandmother and my father, when he was mad. It made me cringe every time I heard it. My father defended it, proud to pass on his name. But no one in Connecticut went by a double name; and for the record, I'd never met an Ann Steve or a Mary Bob. Gram, however, had never seemed particularly interested in which name I preferred, and she was not the kind of woman one corrected unless looking for a showdown.

She held my arms out by my sides for a better look, as if she was inspecting a piece of produce. "You're so grown up. What a lovely young lady you've become!"

Under her appraising gaze, I was momentarily glad

my mother had convinced me to wear the sundress (no heels, though—that was where I drew the line; from Memorial Day to Labor Day, my feet donned nothing but a toe ring and flip-flops), and then immediately angry with myself for being glad.

After our inspection, we were forced into an awkward round-robin of hugs until everyone, whether we felt like it or not, had hugged everyone else, and could finally take our seats to engage in even more awkward small talk. For what felt like fifteen minutes, we discussed the car ride from Connecticut. Another fifteen on how hard it was to find good movers. Apparently, Betty Campbell (Gordon remembered her, didn't he? She'd had a son two classes below him at Country Day) had her antique Chippendale "just ruined" by two movers she'd hired last year. I caught my mother's eye across the table and had to stuff down a laugh when she furrowed her brow in mock dismay and threw back a gulp of Chardonnay.

The waitstaff, in regulation black and white, swooped in and out, taking orders, delivering salads, topping off iced tea. I noticed that Gram and Pawpaw called our waiter by name, though he didn't wear a name tag. In return, "Roger" was friendly and deferential to "Mr. and Mrs. MacRae." All part of the social contract down here, I supposed, recalling with some disgust one summer when Gram had complained to Pawpaw that Roberta, the housekeeper, didn't "know her place."

I was peacefully silent and halfway through my chicken cordon bleu, pretending to listen to Virginia drone on about the pride and perils of cheerleading, when I realized Gram was speaking to me.

"Ann Gordon, your father tells me you've decided to follow in his footsteps."

I blinked. What was she talking about?

"To Brown," explained Gram when I didn't respond. "Isn't that where you've decided to go to college?"

"Oh. Well, I hope so," I answered. "I'm applying early, but I won't find out if I'm actually accepted until December."

Ms. Statler, our college counselor at Deerwood, had assured me my grades and legacy standing would make me a shoo-in. Nevertheless, my inspiration bolstered by the fact that Brown now figured in my escape from Alabama, I'd been working on the application essay all summer: *Please define yourself in eight hundred words or less in a way that makes you sound intelligent and funny, academically-minded yet well-rounded, original but not too weird, and all in a way that we haven't already read ten thousand times over.*

"Brown!" exclaimed Aunt Nonny, a smile playing on her perfectly shellacked lips. "Goodness, Gordon, it looks like she's inherited your brains at least!" Aunt Nonny turned to the rest of the table, as if she'd said something terribly amusing.

It was often pointed out by my father's family that

I looked much more like my mother. We had the same wavy, chestnut hair; thin face punctuated by a strong nose; and tall, athletic build. In photographs, I looked almost exactly like she had thirty years ago—quite the opposite of my short, fair-haired father. In fact, my only real MacRae feature was my shockingly pale blue eyes. Comments like Aunt Nonny's always put me on edge, as if it were somehow *my* fault that my mother's genes had won out.

"Well, I don't know that I had anything to do with it, but we're certainly proud of her," my father said, looking not at Aunt Nonny but at Gram. "Annie was on the dean's list every year at Deerwood."

Out of the corner of my eye, I thought I saw Richard smirk. Thanks, Dad, I groaned inwardly.

"How wonderful," was Gram's answer. Then, leaning in close, she lowered her voice as if no one else at the table could hear. "Ann Gordon, I'm sure your father has told you, but your grandfather and I would very much like to do our part for your education."

"Thanks, Gram," I replied, trying, and I feared failing, at sincerity.

The reality was I didn't have much choice. Gram held the purse strings in our family. She came from what I'd once, as a kid, heard my mother call "old money." My grandparents had offered to pay for college. This was appreciated by my parents, who could never have afforded it on their own, but secretly hoping I wouldn't have to rely on Gram and Pawpaw's financial graces, I had applied for a student-athlete scholarship that my field hockey coach at Deerwood told me about. After three years on varsity, two as a starter, she thought I stood a chance.

"We know that college is shamefully expensive, but I strongly believe"—Gram went on, raising her voice, for all the world to hear—"that a good education is absolutely necessary for a young woman these days. It's not like when I was growing up. It was rather remarkable when I decided to continue my studies at Queen Anne's. Isn't that right, dear?"

Pawpaw, with a mouth full of steak, nodded his head from the far end of the table.

Uncle Tripp lightly tweaked me on the arm. "This is gonna be a big year for you, kiddo."

Kiddo? Seriously? My uncle was—"Bless his heart," as they said down here (a kind of get-out-of-jail-free preface to any insult)—the cheesiest but kindest man I'd ever met. He always had a silly grin on his face, like his pig had just won first prize in the county fair, and he was fond of terms like "kiddo" and "buddy."

"I guess so," I answered into my plate. If you want to count being torn from everything near and dear to you and relocated to your own personal nightmare as a "big year."

"Omagosh," Charlotte squealed suddenly, making me think maybe she'd unearthed a diamond in her mound of cheese grits, "you get to *deb* this year! We're gonna be so jealous."

"*So* jealous," Virginia repeated. "We don't get to 'cause Daddy's not the oldest son." She lowered her chin and looked imploringly at her father through her blond bangs. Only Charlotte's braces helped me tell the twins apart these days.

"Well, we'll see, girls," said Aunt Nonny. "Daddy's gonna talk to Mr. Manley at the Heritage Society when the time comes."

I had no idea what my cousins were talking about, but I *did* know that if Virginia stuck her lip out any farther, either she was gonna lose it or I was.

"I'm not so sure the deb would be Annie's cup of tea," my father said hesitantly.

"What's 'the deb'?" I vaguely recalled something about society girls curtsying in white, gossamer gowns—I think I'd seen it in an old movie when I was home sick channel-surfing—but I thought the practice had faded out around the same time as the ice-cream parlor and drive-in theater.

Gram ignored me. "Don't be ridiculous, Gordon," she said with a dismissive flick of the hand. "She's a MacRae. Of course she'll make her debut."

Aunt Nonny reached across the table, lightly pressing

her hand on mine, as though preparing to impart some jewel of wisdom for the ages. "The debutante ball, honey. It's a tradition where 'eligible'"—she made quotation marks with her fingers in the air—"girls, or I should say 'women'"—again with the air quotes—"are presented to society. There's a ball in July, sponsored by the Heritage Society. The Magnolia Ball. It's really quite an honor."

"It used to be so you could find a husband," inserted Virgina, "but now it's just a big party."

Charlotte nodded knowingly, her ponytail bobbing. "Yeah, it's like a wedding, but you're not getting married. You get to wear a long, white dress, like a wedding gown, and you have guys in tuxedos escort you, and you waltz, and you're like, a princess for the night!" she gushed, her eyes so wide with excitement it made me nervous. "It's supposed to be soooo fun!"

"Virginia, it is not just a party," Aunt Nonny clucked, folding her napkin in her lap. "It's for charity. And it really is fun, Annie. I did it when I was eighteen."

"*Presented* to *society?*" I asked, cocking an eyebrow and glancing down the table, waiting for someone to give up the joke.

"Well, it's more of a symbolic thing now." Aunt Nonny nodded. "But it is still quite elegant."

"It's tradition," Gram added, with all the authority expected of a matriarch.

I had opened my mouth to say child brides and

foot-binding were traditions in parts of the world, too, when my mother cut in: "It does sound nice." She shot me a look that said "let me handle this" and then smiled at Gram. "I'm sure there will be plenty of time to settle in before we have to worry about that, though."

Only, my mother was wrong. I didn't plan on settling in—ever. For me, Beaufort was just a pit stop.

"So, that went okay." My mom patted my father's knee as our old, blue Volvo eased out of the Club parking lot and onto a leafy boulevard.

"It did. I don't know why I was worried." He took her hand from his lap and kissed it.

"Hello? Young, impressionable child back here," I reminded them. "Could you please keep the Parental Displays of Affection to a minimum?"

"I'm sorry, dear, you're right," my mother responded with the sarcasm I had also, obviously, inherited from her. "We'll try to reserve just bitter arguing for your presence. We don't want to emotionally damage you with the sight of a functional marriage."

"Thanks. Hey, what was all that stuff about making *mah day-bew*?" I asked, pulling out my best Aunt Nonny impression and causing my mother to laugh despite herself.

"Don't worry," she assured. "It's probably just one night where you have to dress up and talk to Gram's friends. Maybe she'll forget about it."

"Unfortunately," my father sighed as he flicked on the turn signal, "I sincerely doubt that. Debbing is a pretty big deal down here. And Mother's never been one to forget anything."

"Did you deb, Dad?" I loved how it was a verb *and* a noun.

"Well, I wasn't a debutante—that's just for the girls—but I was an escort. Twice."

"Well, ain't no way you're getting me into a big, white dress, curtsying for no Beaufort society. That's just crazy talk."

I wanted to make my position clear from the get-go: I'd be "debbing" over my dead body. I tried to imagine myself in a fluffy gown, descending a crystalline staircase, waving like a newly crowned Miss America. My friends in Connecticut would flip out. In fact, it'd almost be worth it just to see the look on Jamie's face. Almost.

"Well"—my father sounded hesitant—"don't forget, your grandparents are likely the ones paying for college. Gram may ask you to do this in return. . . . But we'll cross that bridge when we come to it."

I redirected the air-conditioning vent at my face and closed my eyes. "That bridge has been come to, crossed, and burned, Dad. Fughedaboudit."

That night I paced my room, my cell phone cradled between my shoulder and ear. Jamie was on the other end, just as she had been every night since we'd gotten phone privileges in sixth grade—except now the call was long distance.

"So guess what my grandmother came out with tonight at dinner?"

"Oh, no! What?" Jamie was already giggling in anticipation.

"She wants me to deb."

"Do what?"

I told her it was just another example of the alternate universe I now lived in.

"Come on, it can't be that bad. What is it?" she pressed.

I picked up a pen and started to doodle nervously on my very blank desk calendar. "Some lame excuse for fun down here. They get all the eighteen-year-old girls—excuse me, 'eligible young ladies'—decked out in white dresses and prance them around for potential husbands at a big ball."

"Seriously? You're going to be auctioned off?" Jamie was cracking up.

"Not exactly auctioned off . . ."

"Can we pool our money and bid on you?"

"Please!" I groaned.

"Yeah, I can't really see you debting."

It was my turn to laugh. Typical Jamie. She'd been my best friend since Mrs. Klostermeyer's third-grade reign of terror, when we'd bonded over our refusal to drink milk at snack time. Jamie was one of those "free spirit" types, full of surprises. And I was the only person she knew who could make her laugh so hard soy milk came out of her nose.

"No, *deb-bing*," I corrected. "Although, my grand-mother probably sees it that way." I scribbled over my sun doodle and started a fresh one.

"What do you mean?"

"Well," I sighed. How to explain this to the girl whose parents owned half of Connecticut but who preferred a broken-down Volkswagen and wore dresses she'd sewn herself?

I told her how Gram had a very irritating way of bringing up the fact that she and Pawpaw were paying for my education without ever being so crass as to just come out and say it. "It's like she's reminding me that I have to play by her rules," I explained.

"*That* is screwed up. Live and let live." Jamie's credo found a way into almost every conversation.

"Yeah, well, everything down here is screwed up," I sighed, abandoning my doodle for the mini snow globe Jamie had sent in her care package. "You know what else is screwed up?" I shook the globe, watching the white flecks swirl around the Manhattan skyline, and hesi-tated because I knew what she was going to say. "I miss Jake."

"Annie . . ." Jamie started.

After nearly six months of obsessing from afar over Jake Hollister's every perfect feature—the hair that confirmed his effortless hotness, the sense of humor that seemed cosmically attuned to my own, the way his pants fell over his hips just so—and another glorious, albeit surprising, six months of admiring up close, the catastrophic had happened. He had cheated on me. The week before I left. And somehow he had found a way to blame it on the fact that *I* was moving. He'd even had some psychobabble explanation to back it up: he was subconsciously pulling away from me so it wouldn't hurt as bad when he lost me, see? My ass. Jake had always had a thing for Michelle Kerner. She was a sophomore and the kind of girl my grandmother might refer to as "loose."

Still, inexplicably, I missed him, as evidenced by the photo I secretly tucked into whatever book currently lay on my bedside table.

"I know! I know!" I cut in before Jamie could object. "I just feel so"—I searched for the words—"so upside down right now. Nothing's clear. And we dated for six months—that's a long time, Jamie! Maybe he's learned his lesson? Maybe we could make it work for a year?" I said this even though, in the pit of my stomach, I knew it wasn't true.

"Don't think about it, Annie. The best thing is just to focus on the here and now." Another of Jamie's catchphrases. "Jake is in Connecticut, and you're in Alabama."

"Yeah, thanks for reminding me," I said.

As if I could have forgotten . . .

THREE

A lady is a cordial neighbor.

Besides a chatty AC repairman and a cable guy whose butt-crack exposure would have put any plumber to shame, we hadn't had many visitors since our arrival in Beaufort, so I was surprised when the doorbell rang the following weekend. Wondering who could possibly feel the need to interrupt my lifelong tradition of Saturday morning game shows, I hauled myself off the couch and shuffled past towers of empty boxes that lined the front hallway, waiting to be recycled. Glancing down, I realized I was still wearing my pajamas. I shrugged; it wasn't like there was anyone here I needed to impress.

Unlatching the chain, I cracked the door and peeked out. A girl my age in a pink polo shirt and khaki capris embroidered with whales was standing on our stoop, a basket in hand. Too old to be a Girl Scout, I noted.

"Hi!" she said enthusiastically, undeterred by the barely open door or the blank expression on my face.

"I'm Courtney. We live across the street. I noticed the moving truck, so I came by to introduce myself."

"Oh. Hi." I squinted in the sunlight as I opened the door wider.

"Omagosh!" Courtney exclaimed, seeing my rumpled pajamas and the bun of unruly, brown hair piled on top of my head. "I hope I didn't wake you!"

I flicked a stray cornflake from my shorts and informed her I was just eating breakfast. Surprisingly, I actually had a full day ahead of me. Field hockey preseason started that afternoon.

"Perfect! I brought you some muffins," Courtney beamed. The smell of warm baked goods wafted from under the checkered dish towel.

"Thanks." I took the basket, but Courtney continued to stand there, blinking and smiling. "Sorry," I said quickly, realizing I hadn't introduced myself. "I'm Annie."

"Nice to meet you, Annie. You're gonna looooove Beaufort," she assured me.

"Great." Unlikely, but it was too early in the morning to argue with the girl.

"What year are you?"

"I'll be a senior at Beaufort Country Day."

She lit up like a Christmas tree. "Me too! That's so fuuuun! But I go to St. Bernard's"—her smile fell into a frown—"but I hope we can hang out sometime. . . ."

"Yeah, that'd be great," I lied. Courtney was beginning to annoy me. Muffins or no muffins, I was missing a rerun of *Who Wants to Be a Millionaire*.

"Alrighty!" Every one of her sentences sounded as if it should end in three exclamation points and a smiley face. "Well, welcome to the neighborhood. See ya 'round!"

Courtney bounced off the brick stoop and down our pathway, looking both ways as she crossed the always-quiet street, and went into a small, Tudor-style house festooned with the biggest, reddest University of Alabama flag I'd ever seen; it could have doubled as a parachute. Closing the door, I returned to Regis with the feeling I'd just been mauled by a one-person pep rally.

Fishing at the bottom of my gym bag, all I came up with was an old Power Bar wrapper. Yuck. Where was my mouth guard? I knew I had put it in there that morning. Around me, the locker room was emptying as girls made their way out to the field, cleats clicking on the white tile floor.

Preseason was the first thing I'd actually looked forward to since arriving in Beaufort. When I played hockey, I could forget where I was, just be in the game. And that was *exactly* what I needed these days.

At Deerwood I'd been a starting forward on the varsity team. Though I'd never been competitive in other aspects of my life, something about stepping onto the field and lining up person-to-person with an opponent brought out a fighting instinct in me. Jamie, never much the athlete, used to tease me about my alter ego, calling me, with a Schwarzeneggeresque Austrian accent, "The Annihilator."

When I told my team at Deerwood about the move south, they'd informed me that no one played hockey in Alabama. "Nope, just cheerleading," they'd said. I'd laughed, but prayed they were joking, and was relieved to learn that Country Day did, in fact, have a team, even if, according to the collection of "Most Improved" ribbons in the gym's trophy case, it sucked.

Finally, my hand grasped what felt like a mouth guard. I pulled out the molded piece of yellow plastic. Tucking it into my shin guard, I threw my bag in the locker and grabbed my stick as I hurried out to the practice field.

Around twenty girls were already arranged in a large circle in the center of the field, chatting and stretching. The words "Roll Tide" screamed across the butt of the short-shorts on a girl standing in the middle. Her brown hair, highlighted within inches of its life, was pulled back into a ponytail, and she had one of those perfect bodies I'd decided could only be the product of genetic mutation. She and a very blond friend were involved in an animated story. I sat to stretch at the outskirts of the circle, trying to look nonchalant, like I was sitting alone by choice, not necessity.

The coach, short and sturdy with a mousy face, clapped her hands for our attention and introduced herself as Miss Applebaum, a senior at Queen Anne's from Boston, who would be subbing for the normal coach while she was out on maternity leave.

"Okay, I'm gonna count you off into offensive-defensive pairs," she barked. "Your partner will also be your warm-up buddy. Offense over here, defense over there."

I went to stand with the offense as Miss Applebaum counted.

"Five," I said, when she pointed at me.

"Find your partner," she yelled over our heads when she was done. "We're taking four warm-up laps before sprints."

The blonde who'd been standing with Short-Shorts in the stretching circle sauntered over to me.

"Hey, I'm Mary Price," she said in a buttery-sweet accent. She had chocolate doe eyes and delicate features accented by two perfect dimples.

We took off jogging, and as our cleats pounded the field, I searched for one of those brainless introductory questions you're obligated to ask after meeting someone new. Mary Price beat me to the punch.

"So you're new here?"

"Yep. My family just moved from Connecticut."

"That's cool . . . I've never been to Connecticut," she added.

"Yeah, it's nice." And by "nice," I meant a lot cooler than Alabama—both figuratively and literally. Sweat was already pooling beneath my shin guards.

"Have you played hockey before?" Mary Price went on when I didn't elaborate.

"I've been playing since I was ten."

"Wow! I only started in ninth grade. I used to dance —ballet—but it got too competitive so I started playing sports instead." She laughed at the incongruity of her statement.

I was searching for an appropriate response when Short-Shorts and her partner caught up with us. "So, Applebutt seems like a load of fun," Short-Shorts said sarcastically.

Mary Price pointed to me. "Y'all, this is Annie. Annie, the rude girl is Mary Katherine, and that's Bess."

"Hey," the girls said in unison.

"You're new," Mary Katherine stated matter-of-factly. I nodded at the astute observation. "Where you from?"

"Connecticut."

My answer was met with a thoughtful silence that made me wonder whether Mary Katherine even knew where Connecticut was. She finally grunted a "huh" before continuing with more choice observations about Miss Applebaum.

The drills we had to do were simple—mostly ball control stuff I'd mastered in middle school. Mary Price was a decent player, not great. She had most of the skills down and made up for any lack by being fast. All that running, thankfully, didn't leave much time for chitchat, but all too soon it was time for cooldown. Mary Price and I were stretching our hamstrings when Mary Katherine and Bess flopped down next to us.

"Y'all . . . seriously, I think I'm gonna throw up if I have to run another sprint." Mary Katherine's face was bright red.

"Serves you right." Mary Price laughed. "MK only works out when bribed or coerced, which is totally unfair considering she has a *Maxim* body," she informed me. "She plays defense so she doesn't have to run as much."

"Shut up. No I don't. And I have love handles. But I've turned over a new leaf. I'm gonna be healthy from now on. Exercise and no refined sugar."

"Except Slurpees," Mary Price corrected, switching legs.

"Right. And Krispy Kremes. I *luv* me some Krispy Kremes."

Mary Price rolled her eyes, as I imagined "MK" firing up the deep fryer. That's what they did down here, right? Deep-fried everything they could get their hands on, while still maintaining bodies that inspired Daisy Dukes.

"Omagosh, y'all!" Bess interjected so unexpectedly I jumped. "Did y'all see last night's *Ocean Drive*? First of all, Jessica M. is like, so ano."

I hadn't gotten into the California teen-model reality show. It pained me to watch the sobbing confessionals and drunken, night-vision grope-fests. In fact, one of the contestants had gone to Deerwood. The rumor mill had not been kind to her, and while I could have impressed these girls with my insider information, something stopped me from joining in their gab circle. I wasn't a gossip girl. Nor did I intend to become one to win friends and influence people down here. So, while Bess and Mary Katherine expounded on the finer points of Jason K.'s ambiguous sexuality, I tuned out and wondered, instead, what was happening at home—my real home, in Connecticut.

FOUR

A lady introduces herself in new company.

After two weeks of helping my mother—the experienced New Yorker who prided herself on maximizing small spaces—locate the perfect spot for every painting, vase, pillow, and piece of furniture, our new house was cozy and cute, and I couldn't hide there anymore. Which was why I found myself in Aunt Nonny's car, pulling into the drop-off circle at what would be my new alma mater.

A cluster of attractive brick buildings situated on a sprawling carpet of groomed greens in the middle of town, Country Day didn't look so different from Deerwood. While this should have reassured me, it instead inspired a rush of intense homesickness.

Despite my vain attempts at tuning them out, for the entire ride I had listened to Charlotte and Virginia insist loudly from the backseat that Caroline had told Marcy who'd told them that they *had* to be dropped off at the main entrance and not at the senior parking lot.

This was imperative. I didn't have the heart to tell them that their attempt at looking cool on their first day of high school was already futile, as they were dressed in matching sundresses—Charlotte's blue stripes on a yellow background to Virginia's yellow on blue. Having been through three years of high school already, I liked to think I knew the "dos and don'ts" that governed the transformation from tweenhood to teendom. Dressing to match anyone, especially your twin, fell squarely within the "don't" category. Unless, of course, the rules were drastically different down here, which, I realized, was a distinct possibility.

"Thanks, Aunt Nonny," I said as soon as the car stopped and I could catapult myself out of the passenger seat of the massive SUV.

"Thanks, Mom," the twins chimed in unison.

"Sure, honey." Aunt Nonny smiled beneficently at me. "Good luck, girls!" she called after the twins. "Pick you up at three thirty!"

They didn't hear her. Backpacks slung over one shoulder—*so* middle school—Charlotte and Virginia were bouncing off toward a flock of girls, obviously freshmen, hanging out by the bike rack. Remembering how nervous and excited I'd been on my own first day of high school, I could imagine their anxious twittering. At least *that* was behind me, I thought with a sense of relief as I walked past them and up the steps of a large, brick building—Brady Hall, according to the stone inscription over the open double doors. Then it hit me: I might not have to face being a high school freshman again, but, worse, I was now the proverbial Connecticut Yankee in King Arthur's Southern Court.

Down the hall, I could see into a row of spacious, empty classrooms. The dry-erase boards were shiny and clean, and there was the faint plastic smell of new carpeting that was both familiar and off-putting.

In an office to the left, a rather large woman with tightly permed brown hair and an unfortunate mole was fielding calls at a switchboard. She looked like someone who might be able to tell me where to go.

"Hi. I'm looking for the registrar's office. To pick up my schedule?" I hadn't intended it to, but it came out as a question.

"One second, darlin'."

The woman held up one pudgy index finger and pushed a flashing button on the switchboard with another. "Beaufort Country Day," she said in a honeyed voice that raised just slightly at the end, as if "day" were a two-syllable word.

As the woman tried an extension for the caller, I examined her cluttered desk. Plastic figurines, the kind I used to get in Happy Meals, lined the front edge. There were half a dozen photos in homemade frames decorated with sequins, ribbons, and stuff I remembered from my arts and crafts days at camp as "rickrack."

"Sorry, sweetie. What can I do for you?" The woman was off the phone and smiling up at me warmly.

"I'm a new student," I tried again. "I was wondering where I could pick up my schedule."

"Oh sure, hon. Out this door and to the left. There's a sign that says 'MacRae Hall.' That's the administrative offices."

Of course it was. I sighed and headed back through the double doors.

Other than a foreign-exchange student from Düsseldorf, I was the only upperclassman on the new-student tour. Staying toward the back, I turned it into a people-watching exercise, like going to the zoo to see an exotic Southern species roam its natural habitat. As I observed the girls greeting each other, I tried to dissect Country Day's social hierarchy. A prolonged, energetic "heyyya!" suited those acquaintances one socialized with at school but certainly hadn't seen over the summer. A casual, to-the-point "hey" was reserved for close friends, who, as you'd seen them just yesterday, didn't require all the excitement. High-pitched shrieking, hugging, and jumping up and down indicated a friend whose dearness had increased relative to her physical distance over the summer, as it was usually followed by the question "How was the beach/camp/France?"

Much to my surprise and relief, outwardly at least, I didn't stick out as much as I'd anticipated. I didn't know what I'd been expecting—a sea of Lilly Pulitzer hoopskirts?—but the wardrobe of Country Day's student body largely resembled that of Deerwood, perhaps a little heavier on the Crew.

My own style was "preppy hippie," or "prippie," as it was known at Deerwood. While our group hovered on the food chain somewhere just below the other p's (pretties, players, and thoroughbred preppies), by acting like we didn't care about so-called popularity I guess you could say we maintained our own aura of slacker cool. By playing hockey, I'd also kept one foot in the athlete circle. I was "mixed race." But, I reminded myself, my status at Deerwood had no bearing here.

Nor had it helped this morning. It had taken me far longer than I would've admitted to pick out a first-day outfit, finally opting for a flowered, empire-waist top over standard-issue khaki skirt. Probably the only thing distinguishing me from the Country Day girls was my jewelry. I loved jewelry, lots of it, especially rings. My favorite was a large turquoise one Jamie had given me after her parents took her to a Navajo reservation in fifth grade. It had barely left my hand since then, and I had developed a bad habit of spinning it on my finger when I was nervous.

* * *

I was spinning it wildly later that morning when, despite all my impassioned pleas to the universe, time did not stop, speed up, or wrinkle, and eventually I found myself facing that most dreaded part of any first day—lunch. Standing in line at the salad bar, waiting for the rail-thin girl in front of me to finish handpicking every piece of iceberg, I scanned the room and gauged my seating options. There were none—at least none I'd feel comfortable plopping down in with my tray. In a roomful of people, I was shipwrecked on a deserted island.

The senior section was clearly at the far end of the cafeteria, by the drink machines. Almost every table already had people seated around it. The inhabitants of one in particular stood out: Mary Katherine and Mary Price, or "the Marys" as everyone on the hockey team referred to them.

From a mile away you could tell that these were the "pretties." Mary Price Harding's shiny, blonde hair fell to the middle of her back. She was beautiful and tiny, her only flaw that her boobs were smaller even than my own (which, I was the first to admit, were nonexistent). Were she cast in a movie, Mary Price would have played "Popular Girl Number One." Mary Katherine Reynolds wasn't as pretty, but she made up double in the chest department what Mary Price lacked. As I'd passed by the rec room earlier (or WRECK ROOM, as the charming handmade sign taped to the door said), I'd seen her perched on some guy's lap, laughing like she wanted people to notice.

Joining the Marys were two girls: a blonde, bigger than the rest of them (which wasn't saying much), with a wide, open face and large, almond-shaped eyes; and a cute brunette who reminded me of Snow White. (It occurred to me she was the first fellow brunette I'd seen in an astonishingly long time. Either Beaufort had an excess of Scandinavian chromosomes in its gene pool, or there were some very busy hair colorists in this city.) A curly-haired boy in a baseball cap stood at the end of the table, chatting with them.

At the drink machines, I was only ten feet from their table. As I got my glass of water and some Dr Pepper rip-off called Mr. Pibb, I couldn't help but overhear their conversation.

"Shut up, Robert," Mary Katherine's raspy voice commanded. "You did not."

"I did. I swear. Scout's honor," the curly-haired boy said with a laugh.

"Well, I'll believe it when I see it," said Mary Price. Only, phonetically, it sounded more like "*Ahh'll buhleve it when ahh see it*." What was it these people had against enunciation?

So busy eavesdropping, I wasn't expecting Mary Price to glance up from the table and find me watching them, tray in hand. Our eyes met as a flash of recognition passed between us—*Annie from Connecticut*, I could almost read on her face—and for a moment, it seemed she was going to ask me to join them. I'd had enough small talk for a day, so before Mary Price could speak, I broke away and headed for the brick patio behind the cafeteria. At least eating by myself, I could be Annie. Not Ann Gordon. Not Annie from Connecticut. Just Annie, period.

Six classes down, one to go. Yet I stood planted like an idiot in the middle of the hallway. It was 2:43 and I couldn't find my 2:45 English class. The schedule in my hand was no help, as apparently the numbers had disappeared from all the doors on the second floor of the language building. I felt like a contestant on one of the old game shows. Should I pick Door Number One, Door Number Two, or Door Number Three? They all looked the same: a nice, institutional beige color. Door Number One? Tell her what she's won, Chuck! Congratulations, Annie, you've won a year's supply of people you don't know, have nothing in common with, and probably won't like!

"Hey. You lookin' for a class?"

The game show scenario playing itself out in my head was suddenly interrupted by a familiar voice, a guy's. Startled, I turned to find the curly-haired boy from the lunchroom standing behind me. He was wearing baggy khakis and a T-shirt peeking from underneath a tucked-in, navy polo shirt. His hat was now in his back pocket, and his dark curls were hanging almost into his eyes.

"Yeah," I answered, shifting my ten-pound Shakespeare anthology from one arm to the other. "AP English."

He glanced down at my useless yellow schedule. "That's down here. I've got it too. Follow me." He started down the hall in the dictionary definition of an amble. "You new?"

"Yeah. I'm Annie."

"Pleasure to make your acquaintance, Annie," he said slowly, turning his head to offer a smile. He had amazingly green eyes and the longest eyelashes I'd ever seen on a boy. "You got a last name?" he asked.

"MacRae." At the pace we were walking, I was afraid we wouldn't make it to class in time for the final exam, but I didn't want to seem rude and scurry ahead of him. Besides, I didn't know where I was going.

"Robert Lee," he said, introducing himself. I laughed before I saw he was serious.

"I don't suppose your middle name starts with an E?" I joked.

"Funny. Never heard that one before."

I couldn't tell if he was being sarcastic or not. He said everything so . . . lazily.

At the classroom door, Robert stepped aside. I hesitated, not understanding that he was letting me go first, until he swept his arm in a circle that said "After you." Was this what they meant by Southern gentleman?

"Thanks," I whispered and slid into the nearest desk.

The teacher, an older, gray-haired man in a coat and tie named Mr. Smith, according to my schedule, gave me a disapproving glance and continued roll call. "Robert Lee."

"Here."

"Campbell Long."

"Here."

"Ann Gordon MacRae."

"It's Annie, actually."

Again with the freaking name! This had happened in almost every class today. I was shackled to the double name like a ball and chain.

"You're a new student?"

"Yeah." I nodded.

"Where have you transferred from, Miss MacRae?" Mr. Smith was peering at me over wire-rimmed glasses.

"Deerwood Academy. In Connecticut."

"I'm familiar with Deerwood. Welcome. And for future reference, in this classroom, we answer questions with 'Yes' and 'No, sir.'"

I bristled and blushed at the same time. I thought I had signed up for AP English, not the military. Was the man going to tell me to drop and give him twenty next?

"Bliss Meyers," he said, instead.

"Here," a soft voice replied.

Turning, I recognized Snow White from the lunch-room. Up close she was even prettier. Her hair was perfectly straightened and her makeup flawless. The open collar of her tight, purple polo shirt revealed pearls, while her sandblasted denim skirt gave new meaning to the term "mini." She'd even gone to the effort of finding matching purple flip-flops.

"James Smalley." Mr. Smith's voice rang out again.

"Present, *sir*," a round boy with an unruly mop of sandy hair piped from the back row. A laugh rippled through the class, and Mr. Smith gave Mr. Smalley a look that said simply, *I am not amused.*

Roll concluded, Mr. Smith began to pace the length of the blackboard. "Well, I assume you've all completed your summer reading," he said, his fingers steepled condescendingly in front of him. "If not, you have no place in this class. So, without further ado, who can tell me what the green light at the end of Daisy's dock symbolizes?" He turned abruptly, his chin raised slightly as he peered at us from the front of the classroom.

I knew this. Embarrassingly enough, I'd discussed this very question with my father. *The Great Gatsby* was one of my favorite books, and my dad, who wrote his thesis on social criticism in modern American literature, had lured me into a conversation over dinner one night.

I ignored the impulse to raise my hand and was surprised when Robert Lee did instead.

"Yes, Mr. Lee?"

"Money, envy, the American Dream."

"Very good."

Chivalrous, cute, *and* smart. I was impressed. Maybe slow didn't equal stupid. And maybe, just maybe, the South would have a few perks after all. . . .

I had been waiting for my mom by the senior parking lot for exactly five minutes, which was five minutes too long, by my watch. In that seemingly short period of time, the entire senior class of Beaufort Country Day had passed me sitting alone on a bench. I thought Bliss had smiled as she passed, but not sure it was intended for me, I had pretended not to see and instead nervously rifled through my backpack for nothing in particular.

Why did I care, I asked myself, what these people thought? They didn't even know me! I wasn't debs and deep-fried doughnuts, fake manners, and cheerleading. I was a Connecticut girl, prippie, starting forward for Deerwood Academy varsity field hockey. *One year*, I mentally reassured myself as I sat alone on the wooden bench. That was my new mantra. One year, and I would be on my way to Brown, safely on the right side of the Mason-Dixon, and back to where I was Annie, not Ann Gordon.

My internal pep talk was interrupted by the startling sound of a loud car horn. A shiny, red pickup wheeled through the parking lot, leaving black skid marks and a puff of exhaust in its wake. The horn was actually a honking version of the song "Dixie," and the driver was James Smalley from AP English. On the truck bed, two boys struggled to keep their balance and waved their shirts over their heads, woohoo-ing as if they were at a football game.

Oh. My. God, I thought, wishing I had a camera. Exhibit A. Where *I* came from, this kind of stuff only happened in movies.

Blessedly, I was saved from Beaufort's own Dukes of Hazzard when my mother pulled up in the Volvo.

"Hey, baby, looking for a date?" she asked, leaning out the window.

"Funny," I said, getting into the car and shutting the door a little harder than was necessary.

"How was your first day among the Others?"

"Don't even ask."

"How are things down there?" Jamie ventured later that night. "Unbearable?"

I lay on my bed, butt pushed up against the wall, legs extended above my head, staring at the Bob Dylan poster I'd just managed to tape to my ceiling. Due to the ever-present humidity, one corner was already peeling, threatening to take the rest of Bob with it.

Jamie had been filling me in on first-day Deerwood gossip: Bodie had gotten a new car; Caitlin Watson had gotten a new nose ("deviated septum"); and the freshmen didn't know how to respect their elders. (They should sic Mr. Smith on 'em, I thought.)

I'd been holding back on my pity party, sure Jamie was sick of hearing me whine. But since she'd asked . . .

"You have no idea," I moaned. "I mean, it's not *that* different from Deerwood. It's pretty preppy. But it's the little things. I saw a guy wearing a Confederate flag belt buckle. And they served okra at lunch. Have you ever *had* okra, Jamie?"

"What's okra?"

"I don't know, a vegetable or something. It was fried beyond recognition. I steered clear."

Jamie gave a distracted laugh. "Hang on a sec, okay?"

I heard the thump of her hand covering the phone and two muffled voices. I twirled my ring.

"Hey," she said, coming back. "Actually, Gina and Beth just got here. We're meeting the guys in the park. Can I call you back later?"

Which guys, I wondered. Would Jake be there?

I had a flashback: Jake's shaggy, brown hair hanging characteristically into his eyes as he sailed a Frisbee through the air to Bodie—or was it Matt? He had been barefoot that day, one of our last together. He had kissed me when no one was looking. The memory made my stomach tighten.

"Sure," I told Jamie. "We can talk later."

"Thanks, babe. Later," she said, hanging up before I could say good-bye.

I stared up at my ceiling. It was just me and Bob now.

FIVE

A lady can give and take a compliment.

If I had suspected okra would be the worst of my fish-out-of-water experiences, I would have been dead wrong. I was now headed, per my father's stern orders, to the annual Grace Children's Hospital/Junior League Honor Luncheon at the Beaufort Women's Club with Gram. Junior League. Honor Luncheon. Women's Club. I couldn't have made this stuff up if I'd tried. Jamie had almost peed her pants when I told her.

Gram's huge, silver Cadillac (license plate: "GMM III" for Gordon Marshall MacRae, the Third, thank you very much) was idling in our driveway. As I passed my mom in the hall on my way out, I shot her the biggest "woe is me" look I could muster.

"Oh, don't be so dramatic, Annie," she said. "You're going to a luncheon, not the guillotine. I know she's overbearing, but one day you'll wish you'd spent more time with her."

"Doubtful," I said, plodding down the carpeted stairs and out the door.

Gram was reapplying her coral lipstick in the rear-view mirror when I opened the car door. She gave me her signature up-and-down glance, dropped her lipstick in her purse, and snapped it shut with a crisp click.

"Is this what you're wearing?"

"Yeah. I mean, yes, ma'am. Is there something wrong with it?"

I looked down at my outfit, making sure the knee-length skirt with light blue, button-down shirt, and pointy tan heels borrowed from my mom had not, magically, from the house to the car, morphed into booty shorts and go-go boots. Without an emergency trip to Ann Taylor LOFT, this was the most ladylike outfit I had been able to pull together.

"Where are your stockings?"

"It's not that chilly. I'm okay," I assured her as I started to step into the front seat. It was barely fall, for crying out loud. The trees in our front yard hadn't even dropped their leaves yet.

"It's about what's appropriate, Ann Gordon, not the temperature. Why don't you go inside and put on a pair of stockings?"

Her tone told me it was a command, not a request.

After shielding my legs from the outside world with a

pair of my mother's thin, practically invisible, and totally useless stockings, I soon found myself following Gram into the Beaufort Women's Club. A brass plaque at the entrance told me that the historical house had been renovated and dedicated in 1924, under the patronage of a Mrs. John Cady Merriweather, Jr. I was still slightly confused, as we crossed the immaculately decorated foyer, as to what sort of "women" things went on in the Women's Club. On this particular occasion, Gram had explained, the League and hospital were recognizing young area women who had shown exceptional volunteerism at their respective high schools. Followed, I imagined, by makeovers and a pillow fight.

Sunlight poured through the ballroom's floor-to-ceiling windows, throwing rainbows off the crystal chandeliers. Past the name-tag station (mine, of course, read "Ann Gordon"), a sea of Gram look-alikes mingled among tables set with glittering silverware and extravagant flower arrangements. Interspersed among the old ladies and middle-aged women were girls who must have been about my age but looked ten years older, thanks to their prematurely donned stockings and suits.

Gram waved to a few ladies across the room before accosting a woman named, according to the name tag that drooped alarmingly close to her belt, Bitty Carlyle.

"Bitty!" Gram shouted into the old woman's ear. "I'd like you to meet my granddaughter, Ann Gordon

MacRae. You remember my son, Gordon?"

"Who?" Bitty asked loudly. The poor woman was obviously confused not just as to who Gordon was, but who this woman in front of her was, too.

But Gram persevered. "Gordon. My son. This is his daughter, Ann Gordon."

Delicately, I shook Bitty's withered hand. "Hi. Nice to meet you," I said, careful to enunciate each syllable.

"Oh hello, dear," she croaked, a glimmer of comprehension coming to her milky eyes. "You're the one who caught young Gordon? Do you two have any children yet?"

Repulsed at the thought, I struggled for a response.

"Ann Gordon, why don't you get us some punch?" Gram stepped in. Only, once again, it was a command, not a request.

I nodded and eagerly slipped away to the beverage table, where pineapple slices floated in a cut-crystal bowl filled with sparkling, pink punch. When I returned, two glasses in hand, Bitty had moved on. Handing a glass to my grandmother, I surveyed the bustling room, which was by now a flurry of chatter.

"Ann Gordon," Gram said in a quiet, even voice, "'Hi' may be how you address your peers, but these ladies expect a proper greeting. 'Hello' or 'How do you do?' would be more polite." She sipped her punch.

I was too stunned to react. "How do you . . . do?"? What was this, *My Fair Lady*? Bitty had thought I was procreating with my own father; I sincerely doubted she was taking notes on the propriety of my salutations. But already another of Gram's "dear friends" had descended upon us.

The succession of elderly women dressed in crisp suits and heirloom pearls seemed never ending. I had the sinking realization that Gram, as a member of the children's hospital board, and by extension I, as her guest and granddaughter, were expected to speak with each and every one of them, inquiring after their husband/children/cats and agreeing on the wonderful increase in turnout from last year's luncheon. Never mind the fact I was not at last year's luncheon.

Gram's enthusiasm was unwavering, while I, on the other hand, was using every ounce of willpower I possessed not to glance at my watch. Henry "How do you do?" Higgins would have had a coronary at that. I introduced myself properly to each of the ladies, smiling until my cheeks ached and trying not to stare at the hot-pink lipstick on Mrs. Chapman's false teeth.

The whole thing was so exhausting that I was actually relieved when I recognized Courtney, the one-woman welcoming committee from across the street, and another girl, vaguely familiar, approaching me.

"Annie! I'm so glad you caaaame!" Courtney gushed

in her ongoing campaign for Miss Congeniality. "This is Taylor."

Up close, I recognized Taylor as the girl who usually sat with the Marys and Bliss at lunch.

"Hi." Taylor grinned beneficently. I wanted to tug on Gram's elbow and point out that *she* had said "Hi."

"I'm Annie. Nice to meet you." Shaking Taylor's hand, I thought how bizarre it was that teenagers did that down here. In Connecticut, shaking another kid's hand would immediately put you on the Weird List.

"Annie goes to BCD," Courtney added.

"Oh! Me too!" said Taylor. Like Courtney, she also spoke with extreme punctuation. "Are you in the Junior League, too?! We just joined as provisional members!"

"Oh, no," I replied, trying not to show my absolute horror at the idea. "My grandmother is involved with the hospital. I just moved here."

Hearing herself mentioned, Gram turned her attention from a blond woman in a green dress. "Hello, girls. Ann Gordon, would you please introduce me?" she asked, shining a regal smile upon Courtney and Taylor.

I had the fleeting urge to introduce them as Paris and Britney, but I bit my tongue. "Gram, this is Courtney and Taylor. This is my grandmother."

"Mary Randolph MacRae. Pleased to meet you. You girls are being honored today?"

"Yes, ma'am," they chimed in harmony.

"Isn't that wonderful," she said, then looking at me, added, "I thought this might be a good opportunity for Ann Gordon to meet some of the girls she'll be making her debut with."

I was annoyed, first of all, that Gram was talking about me as if I wasn't there and, secondly, that she so slyly assumed I'd be making my debut. Hadn't we covered this already? Besides, Gram couldn't even introduce me to her friends; how did she expect to introduce me to society? She smiled between the two Southern specimens and me, no doubt comparing us on some mental checklist.

I was saved only by the sound of a knife clinking against glass. A woman stood at a microphone on a dais at the end of the room, waiting for quiet before beginning her prepared words of welcome.

Taylor gave my arm a light pat. "It was nice to meet you, Ann Gordon."

"You, too," I said.

"By the way, I loooove your skirt," Courtney whispered.

"Oh, thanks," I said, mildly surprised. "It's actually really old."

There was a strained moment of silence. Then Courtney winked and added, "Well, it's adorable," before skittering off behind Taylor.

As Gram and I searched for our names on the tiny,

calligraphied place cards that dotted the tables (not the brightest idea when you had a roomful of half-blind old women), she again whispered in my ear. "Ann Gordon, it's impolite to reject a compliment."

"I wasn't rejecting it! This skirt *is* old. I've had it for like, three years," I whispered back.

"Regardless," Gram said, finding our names and taking her seat.

"Jeez. I thought modesty was a virtue," I mumbled as I plopped down next to her.

Gram cut her eyes at me sideways, then focused her attention on the stage, where a woman was embarking on a speech about bake sales and fund-raising goals. She had the thickest accent I'd ever heard. Unable to understand nearly a word of what she was saying, I tried to follow the crowd's cues for applause, but by now my stomach was rumbling, making it difficult. I hadn't eaten since cornflakes with *Family Feud*.

When the speech was over and everyone had turned to their sweet tea and salads, Gram turned to me. "Ann Gordon, I'd like you to meet someone," she said, resting her hand gently on the shoulder of the woman seated on her other side. The woman was round in that middle-aged way. Her hair was waved like a fifties sitcom mom, and she wore a hideous scarf knotted beneath her two chins. "This is Totty Patterson, head of this year's debutante committee."

"Hello. It's very nice to meet you," I recited in English so perfect that it would have made the Queen proud.

Gram gave Totty Patterson a quick rundown of my life, impressing the facts that I was her granddaughter, Gordon's daughter, an A-student, and evidently "very involved" (whatever that meant—as far as I knew, Gram had no idea what my extracurriculars included). Midway through my résumé, it hit me. Glancing around the room at the smiling young girls and appraising matrons, I realized this wasn't just an Honor Luncheon; it was an undercover debutante rush. This was a look-see at the new crop for the old debutantes, a chance to give potential debs their seal of approval. I almost gasped. Gram was totally pimping me out! I tried to maintain an air of normalcy as I answered Mrs. Patterson's questions, but now I was not only starving, I was pissed off.

By the time the soup arrived, I was hungry and angry enough to eat mine and everyone else's at the table, although I suspected reaching across and plunking my spoon into Totty Patterson's bowl would have been frowned upon. Finally out of the spotlight, I was pretending not to think of my deb induction and trying to enjoy my bisque when Gram leaned over and very quietly asked me not to slurp.

Now, I may not be Miss Manners, but I am also not a heathen who needs to be told how to sip her soup. The rage that bubbled up in me this time was enough to completely ruin my appetite. I quietly fumed for the rest of lunch, speaking only when spoken to and barely touching my quiche. In fact, it took a great deal of self-control not to teach Gram a lesson by abandoning all use of cutlery and eating with my bare hands.

Back in the car, an icy silence descended between us. What ticked me off even more than my grandmother's ridiculous needling and thinly veiled marketing ploy was that Gram was either oblivious to the utter contempt I was quietly channeling her way, or she was taking the so-called "high road" and ignoring me as if I were a child. Either way, it was infuriating. I stared out the Cadillac's window, squinting my eyes in the glare of the afternoon sun and trying to calm myself by counting the number of American flags stuck in yards, run up flagpoles, and planted above doorways.

Finally, Gram spoke. "It's good for you to get to know these girls, Ann Gordon. Some of them will be making their debut, too."

She might as well have taped the message to a brick and thrown it through my window: YOU'RE DEB MEAT.

"Were you involved in a service society of any kind in Connecticut?" Gram continued.

"No." I stared ahead, determined to communicate my scorn through silence.

"No, ma'am," she corrected. "Ann Gordon, you have to remember that adults are answered with 'sir' and 'ma'am.' It was a good thing poor Bitty Carlyle couldn't hear you, because she would have been offended." Gram said this with sincere distress.

"I'm sorry, ma'am, that I just don't fit in down here," I answered through a clenched jaw. "I didn't really have time for finishing school in Connecticut," I added under my breath.

Gram didn't miss a beat. Her voice was deadly cold. "Of course, dear, it's not your fault that you were brought up in a place where manners are not taught or appreciated. But you live in Beaufort now, and I don't believe it's too much to ask that you at least try and act like it. Especially after all we do for you. . . ." She dangled the last sentence over my head.

It was the last either of us spoke on the rest of a very long, very slow, ride home.

It was official. I *had* to get that scholarship.

SIX

A lady knows which team to cheer for at a sporting event.

"Ann Gordon MacRae, your presence is requested in my office."

Uh-oh, I thought. Dad was using The Full Name, and he was calling me to his "office," the large, windowless closet he'd filled with an old desk and his bookshelves. As I shuffled down the hall from my bedroom, I quickly searched my mind for anything I'd done lately that could possibly warrant usage of The Full Name.

Nothing. I was an angel child these days. Proof positive? It was five o'clock on Friday night and I was in my pajamas. How could I even have a chance to get into trouble when my life sadly consisted of home, hockey, and school? Had Gram complained about the luncheon? Doubtful. She was mean, but, as she once told me, "a true lady never tattles." Could I have left a drink sitting perilously close to the computer again? Not that I remembered. Were the clothes that covered my floor finally spilling into the hall? My parents had been surprisingly lax about my keeping my room clean since the move, as if a cease-fire on that harassment could make up for the fact that they'd ruined my life.

"What's up?"

My father looked up from the papers strewn over his cluttered desk.

"Got your cell phone bill today. Care to venture a guess as to how many overtime minutes you racked up last month?"

"Ummm . . ."

"Three hundred and sixteen."

"Whoops."

Gazing down at my Tweety Bird slippers, I bit my lip apologetically. I was usually careful, but now that the phone was my primary link to my past life, I'd kind of thrown caution to the wind. Besides, my parents were the ones who had put me in this Southern solitary; the least they could do was pay for my calls to the outside world.

"Really, Dad, I'm sorry. I didn't realize I was talking that much. I'll be really careful from now on."

He took off his glasses, ran a hand through his hair, and gave me a look of exasperation.

"Yes, you will. But that's not what worries me so much, Annie. I know you're still adjusting"—Oh no, I sensed a heart-to-heart coming on—"but with the amount of time you spend on the phone and computer with Jamie, how do you expect to make new friends here? I am beginning to worry about you. You spent your eighteenth birthday watching movies with us. I like to think we're good company, but we can't be *that* fun."

"I know, Dad," I said impatiently, remembering my birthday evening. Sushi at Sue-She Café (evidently the locals found that cute), followed by a romantic comedy with my parents would perhaps go down in history as the most depressing night of my life.

"I just miss everyone in Connecticut," I said, leaning in the doorway.

"Haven't you met some kids at school?"

"God, you make me sound like a total loser! Of course I've *met* people. But not anyone I'd like, call up to hang out with. I don't have anything in common with these people, Dad."

"*These people*? That'll make you friends real fast!"

"I don't need friends; I already have some." They just happened to be in Connecticut, while I was being held against my will in Alabama.

"Nonny called. . . ." he started, absentmindedly sliding the chipped Brown coffee mug he used as a pencil holder two inches to the right.

"Yeah?" I asked hesitantly. What did Aunt Nonny have to do with this conversation?

"She was hoping you might take the twins to a movie later tonight."

"Uh-uh!" I protested, throwing up my hands in a "no way, no how" gesture.

"Why not?" My father seemed honestly perplexed that I hadn't jumped up and down at the prospect. "You used to love playing with them."

My eyes nearly bugged out of my head. "You must be thinking about your *other* daughter. Charlotte and Virginia were whiny and spoiled and told on me when I *wouldn't* play with them."

"It's just a movie, Annie."

He was not seeing the point. My hands moved to my hips. "They're annoying, Dad."

"It's at the mall—you can shop while they see the movie. Aunt Nonny just wants someone there, in case."

I looked past him, at the bookshelf lined with books so old and loved their spines were cracked, and considered this. The truth of the matter was, while my cousins were completely irritating, the boredom that had begun to set in was worse. A night out on the town—or as close as one could come in Beaufort—might be the answer.

My father saw me starting to crack. "It will be your payment for the cell phone bill," he said. He had me there.

"Fine," I groaned, throwing back my head in defeat.

As I padded back to my room to change into jeans, I couldn't help but call back to him, "Will you just let me know when you're off the computer? Jamie said she saw an e-Saver to New York."

Anchored by an Outback Steakhouse and a department store, the Beaufort Galleria Mall glowed in the Alabama night. To hear the twins talk about it, the mall wasn't just a place for shopping; it was a destination in and of itself.

Seriously?—I did a mental check as I followed Virginia and Charlotte into the stucco suburban monstrosity— I was going to *hang out* at the Beaufort Galleria Mall with my cousins? And to add insult to injury, I hadn't even been granted the dignity of driving myself. (It was a feud I'd had with my parents since sophomore year. They said I'd get a car in college, which I saw as one more reason to speed through this year and get on with it.) The pathos of the entire situation was worthy of an ancient Greek tragedy. I was *this* close to plucking out my own eyes.

Entering through the food court, the twins insisted on walking ten feet in front of me, which was fine by me, as I wasn't exactly there for the company either. Occasionally they would giggle, turn to peek at me, then go back to whispering in each other's ears. I rolled my eyes. So we were playing this game, were we?

Inside, the mall was crowded and decorated in a nauseating combination of pink and green, so that it looked as if a watermelon had exploded all over the walls and floors. The food court was checkered in large coral-and-lime squares. Fake palm trees in salmon-colored pots "shaded" the tables, and calypso music jangled over the sound system. I suddenly felt like I was poolside at a Miami retirement community.

Virginia and Charlotte speed-walked past a string of fried-food stalls toward the part of the mall that housed the movie theater. At the ticket window, Virginia finally spun around to face me.

The twins had traded in their matching sundresses for matching designer jeans. Unlike mine, which were baggy and ragged at the hems, theirs hugged their emerging curves and were neatly pressed, no doubt by Aunt Nonny. The pink cardigan Virginia wore hung loosely over her thin frame.

"Annie, we need you to do something for us," she said, as if she were a babysitter speaking to a child, not the other way around.

Charlotte discreetly poked her sister in the ribs. This oughta be good, I thought. What could they so desperately *need* me to do for them?

"We need to see *Dumbass 4*," Virginia continued matter-of-factly, brushing aside her bangs, "but it's rated R."

"Why do you want to see that movie?" I asked, though I already knew I would buy them the tickets, if just to lose them. Virginia's face fell and behind her Charlotte looked stricken.

"Why don't you see that new animated movie, the one with the cute rabbit?" Now I was just messing with them.

"We *have* to see *Dumbass*!" Charlotte suddenly blurted. "Everyone's seen it except us!"

"I haven't seen it." I shrugged.

I could see the gears turning in Virginia's head. Her eyes lit up. "We'll pay for your ticket," she bargained.

What would Aunt Nonny say? Her little belles wanted to watch guys hit themselves in the crotch and eat their own phlegm for two hours *and* were ready to bribe me to help them do it! It would be cruel fun to watch them squirm, but that would mean prolonging this conversation, and I feared they weren't above making a scene.

"I'll get you the tickets," I said, at which point both twins visibly slackened in relief. "Just meet me afterward in the food court. I'm gonna look around. Any good stores here?"

Virginia pondered for a moment, training her blue eyes on her blond bangs, and came up with J. Crew. Charlotte threw in Laura Ashley for good measure. I sighed and figured I could at least browse for two hours.

My shopping excursion was more successful than anticipated. Wandering into a slow corner of the mall by the engraving hut, I'd come across a surfer boutique (curious, as Beaufort was landlocked). I wasn't really a Roxy chick, but some digging had gotten me a cute blue-and-green top.

Satisfied with my purchase, I hunkered down at a greasy, pink table in the food court with my shopping bag and a smoothie. The twins would be done with their gross-out fest in twenty minutes, so I still had some time to kill. I was intently watching a janitor empty a trash can of fast-food wrappers and Styrofoam cups when I heard my name. The first time, I naturally assumed it was another Annie. Who would be shouting *my* name in the Beaufort Galleria Mall?

Then, "Annie!" I heard again, this time recognizing the voice as Mary Price's. I swiveled in my seat to find Mary Price and Bliss speeding across the watermelon food court.

The Marys and I sometimes spoke at hockey practice, usually about our mutual distaste for Applebutt (whose tragic lack of a sense of humor and sadistic love of sprints, not to mention her Northern roots, had doomed her from the beginning). And there was the occasional "hey" in the hallways at school, but, as I'd tried to explain to my dad only hours earlier, ours was a friendship—for reasons beyond his understanding—that was limited to the field. They lived in their world, and I lived in mine.

Consequently, running into Mary Price at the mall,

outside of our established hockey bubble, caught me off guard. It did not, evidently, do the same for Mary Price, because next thing I knew, she was plopping down next to me in the food court, a flurry of excitement. "You'll never *buhleev* who we just saw!" she gushed, her brown eyes glittering.

I glanced at Bliss, but her blank expression gave me no hints. She wasn't exactly the brightest bulb on the chandelier (I had the feeling she'd ended up in AP English by taking a wrong turn on the way to gym), but Bliss seemed nice enough. Although we'd never had a real conversation, she smiled when we passed in the halls. I remembered she borrowed a pen once, and even gave it back after class.

"Who?" I asked, looking once again at Mary Price, stunned by this unexpected barrage of attention.

"APPLEBUTT!" Mary Price almost screamed. "She was totally M.O.ing in front of Outback . . . with a guy!"

Mary Price erupted into hysterics, literally slapping her knees. My mouth fell open—our suspicions about our coach had been wrong. I cracked up as Mary Price tried, between gasps for air, to describe every detail for me: what the guy looked like, what Applebutt was wearing, how far exactly she had been sticking her tongue down his throat. Bliss giggled along.

As our laughter subsided, Mary Price let out a

satisfied sigh. "I'm so glad we saw you. I was *dying* to tell someone, and MK's not answering her phone."

For some reason, Mary Price's last comment deflated my mood. For a split second, part of me wanted Mary Price to be dialing my number at the sight of our hockey coach sucking face with a guy in the Beaufort Galleria Mall parking lot. But that was out of the question. Mary Katherine was Mary Price's best friend, like Jamie was mine.

"What are you guys up to?" I asked, pushing back the odd feeling. Neither of them had shopping bags.

"We're supposed to be seeing a movie, but the boys got hungry. . . . Speak of the devils," Mary Price said abruptly, focusing her attention on a point over my shoulder.

I turned to see Robert Lee and James Smalley, from English, moseying toward us. Smalley's was a nickname of great irony, as he looked like he knew his way around a food court. Poetically, he was now carrying a bucket of fried chicken.

"Hello, ladies," Robert said as he walked up, wiping his hands on a grease-spotted paper napkin.

"Robert, do you know Annie?" Mary Price asked.

His smile was infectious. "I believe I do. She still owes me for the tour I gave her the first day of school." I felt the blood go to my cheeks.

"And this," Mary Price continued the introductions, "is Smalley."

"Hey," I said, inwardly cringing as Smalley tossed a half-gnawed drumstick into the bucket to shake my hand.

"So, Annie," Robert asked, leaning casually on the back of Mary Price's chair, "what brings you to the illustrious Galleria?"

I thought of mentioning the twins, but instead answered "shopping," and pointed at the plastic yellow bag at my feet for proof.

Bliss came to life. "Show us whatcha got!" she squealed, clapping like a little girl on her birthday.

Reluctantly, I pulled my new shirt from its tissue wrapping. I was unaccustomed to these girly rituals. Jamie didn't like shopping and certainly never called for impromptu food court fashion shows.

"Oooh, I love it!" Mary Price gushed, taking the shirt from my hands. "It's kind of . . ." She didn't finish the sentence but held the shirt straight out in front of her for a better look.

"It's kind of prippie," I offered, although I doubted the word had any currency in Alabama.

"Prippie?" Robert repeated, proving me right. He looked at me with one raised eyebrow.

"Preppy hippie," I translated.

He nodded. "Good one." Then, slapping Smalley on the back, he added, "I guess that makes you a prepneck."

"Preppy redneck?" I asked, smiling. He grinned

back, proud at his own inventiveness, and my heart gave a weird thump.

"Well, you're definitely a redneck. . . ." Mary Price said to Smalley, as she stood from the table. "Are y'all done Supersizing yourselves? 'Cause I don't wanna miss the previews."

"Those are the best part," I agreed. I'd always missed the previews, as inevitably, we were running on "Jamie Time."

Mary Price flashed a delighted smile. "That's what I always say."

"You wanna come with us?" asked Robert. "We're seein' *Dumbass*."

"The boys won the coin toss," Bliss explained with a roll of her eyes.

"Yeah, I hear it's getting Oscar buzz," I joked as I saw the twins bounce excitedly into the food court, "but I'm meeting someone, actually."

"Okay. See ya on Monday, then." Mary Price waved as she went.

"We'll let you know how it ends," Robert added with an unexpected wink.

We could hear the loudspeakers from the parking lot behind Country Day's new, state-of-the-art gym. I had thought taking the twins to the mall completed my reparations for the astronomical cell phone bill, but I was sorely mistaken. The next day, my father had guilted me into attending the BCD homecoming football game.

The day was pleasantly crisp and sunny. As we approached, a disembodied voice was announcing the starting lineup, each name followed by wild applause and a small chorus of "boo"s from the direction of the visiting team's bleachers. Reaching the chain-link fence surrounding the field, I noticed a hand-painted banner across the gate had been ripped in two, probably by the pack of players barreling onto the field just moments before. Now it hung limply from either side of the fence, fluttering GET 'EM EBELS in the breeze.

Beaufort's bleachers were a sea of green. A small band struck up a familiar tune as a dedicated cheer-leading squad mashed green-and-white pom-poms and pumped their tan legs in the air, smiling and nodding manically as no one watched. I took a deep breath as my father weaved his way into the stands, searching for a spot to sit.

"How 'bout over there?" he asked, pointing to a sec-tion of bleachers teeming with my classmates, all of whom were rowdy, and some—dare I say it—a little tipsy.

Smalley had his shirt off, revealing a large stomach painted with the words "Go Rebs." As Michael Johnson, apparently our star quarterback, squatted down to receive the snap, Smalley raised his face skyward and howled with such enthusiasm he almost lost his balance and toppled over onto Bliss, sitting next to him. She gave him a playful shove, rolled her eyes, and whispered something to Taylor, of Junior League fame.

"Dad, no. That's the student section," I groaned.

"You're a student," he insisted.

"Why don't we just sit here?"

"Here" was where the old people were relegated. The front row was occupied by team mothers, easily identifiable by the handmade buttons that proudly displayed their sons' faces and numbers.

"You want to sit with the old farts? Annie, to get the full experience you have to sit in the student section!" Before I could protest, my father was excusing himself as he climbed over a group of freshmen to an empty seat in the third row. I had no choice but to follow him—the overarching theme of my life these days.

The game crept by. That was the annoying thing about football—you saw two minutes on the clock, but somehow you'd be there for an hour; unlike field hockey, where time actually meant something. Not even a quarter into the game and I'd already been elbowed twice by some cocky, baby-faced sophomore. "Sorry, darlin'," he said, looking at me bleary-eyed. And just when I thought it couldn't get any worse, my father began belting out a fight song, begun by who else but Smalley.

"Rebels yell, raise some hell!" my father chanted loudly, pumping his fist in the air.

"Dad," I said, alarmed. Were people looking at him? Were people looking at *me* because I was sitting next to him? Not that I should care, but *would he please stop*?!

"Dad!" I said again, louder this time, slumping a little in my seat.

"Yeah?"

"What are you doing?"

He had a huge grin on his face. "Cheering for my old school. I can't believe I remember these songs! You having fun?"

I couldn't help but notice that my father's voice, despite years of successfully suppressing his accent, had taken on a decided twang.

"No," I answered.

"What? It's a tied game! We have a great quarterback this year. I just heard someone say Auburn wants him!" When the oohs and aahs he desired did not pour forth, he added, "That's a big deal around here."

"Yeah, whatever," I said, standing. "I'm going to get a soda. Can I have a couple dollars?"

He distractedly fished for his wallet, handed me a five-dollar bill, and started clapping for a call on the field.

I waded through the stands, like a salmon against the current, and down to the area where the concessions stand was set up: two vacant-looking underclassmen girls sitting at a card table with a cooler full of sodas and a handwritten sign that read SUPPORT BCD BIG PEOPLE FOR

LITTLE PEOPLE, COKES: $2, CANDY: $3. The girl who handed me my Sprite was too busy flirting with a freckle-faced boy propped on the end of the table to get the change right. When I corrected her, she shot me a fierce look, shoved a crumpled dollar bill toward me, and returned her spellbound attention to Connect-the-Dots.

"Thanks," I said sarcastically. Stuffing the bills into my cords pocket as I turned, I didn't notice the girl standing behind me until I ran smack into her. Stumbling back a step, I saw that it was Mary Price.

"Oh, I'm sorry!" she apologized almost reflexively.

Her hair was pulled back in its usual ponytail. The sweater she wore was the same chocolate brown as her eyes, and she had on jeans and cowboy boots—real ones, judging by the caked-on mud and worn-off leather, not the kind Deerwood girls got on Madison Avenue. Mary Katherine was with her. Her yellow polo shirt, over a long-sleeved white tee, was pulled so tight across her chest it looked like the poor horse on the logo was traversing two lemon-colored mountains.

"Hey!" Mary Price said, obviously surprised to see me again so soon. "What's up?"

My honest and obligatory answer was, "Not much."

"I told MK about Applebutt last night."

"I'm so pissed I missed it!" Mary Katherine laughed.

Mary Price cracked open her Diet Coke. "You ready for Tuesday?" she asked me.

71

Tuesday was our first big hockey game against St. Bernard's—Country Day's and, according to the tone of Mary Price's voice, now also my, biggest rival.

"Yeah, I guess."

"We're gonna need you," said Mary Katherine. "Since you're like, All-American."

I blushed. Was she being sarcastic, implying I was cocky? Or was she just being nice? It was hard to tell with Southerners and their Vaseline beauty pageant smiles. Sometimes I couldn't differentiate between cattiness and genuine courtesy.

"No, I'm not," I replied.

Mary Price called me out. "Don't be modest. Yes, you are! You're better than all of us put together."

"Well, thanks." I wasn't sure what else I was supposed to say, so I said good-bye.

"Okay, see ya later." Mary Price smiled. Unlike the manic grin of Courtney Davis, who continued to pop up on my doorstep like a Jehovah's Witness, trying to convert me to Junior League with baked goods, Mary Price's suited her.

I squeezed my way back onto the bleachers and through the crowd, which had swollen significantly during my short absence. As I was pushed and jostled toward my seat, the band struck up a few discordant notes, signaling the end of the first half. Everyone stood and looked expectantly to the field. So I did the same.

A tractor, pulling a platform with hay bales and half a dozen senior guys, puttered down the sidelines, stopping in front of the packed stands.

The boys all wore the same uniform: khaki pants, white button-down shirts, and ties. Like a preppy Kiss cover band, their faces were painted in various designs of green and white. But I quickly recognized Robert Lee under his familiar dingy hat and black curls, spinning a tennis ball inside a long sock over his head. For some reason, it made me think of Jake. The mental image of my ex, with his baggy cargo pants and hemp necklace, attempting this look made me laugh. I'd seen Jake in a tie just once, at his grandfather's funeral, and he'd looked like a dorky little kid on picture day. Mr. Lee, on the other hand, pulled it off effortlessly.

The band played louder as the "cheerleaders" ran back and forth in front of the bleachers, trying to incite a riot. Robert and Ryker, the guy I now knew as Mary Katherine's boyfriend, went to the tractor to pull down four giant cardboard boxes. As they forcefully ripped them open, mountains of miniature plastic footballs spilled onto the sidelines. The boys started lobbing the balls into the crowd, and the bleachers went wild. It was like a scene from the World Series, where spectators trampled women and small children just to claim a foul ball.

Suddenly I got a strange feeling—like someone was

watching me. Someone was. Robert. Before I knew what was happening, he smiled, winked, and threw a perfect spiral pass in my direction. Four freshmen girls in the front row instantly turned with awe and jealousy to see who the lucky recipient had been. Holding the small, plastic ball in my hand, I blushed. Had it really been meant for me? I half expected to turn and see the Marys, Bliss, and Taylor staring me down for stealing their prize. I glanced over my shoulder, but it was obvious I was their last concern. They were too busy laughing at Smalley's clownish thrashing. So the ball was for me?

With the last football passed, the tractor pulled away to make room for the real cheerleaders' halftime show, for which the crowd was markedly less excited.

As the boys left the field, all I could think was, "Hmmm. That was interesting."

SEVEN

*A lady does not debate politics
or religion at the dinner table.*

It was almost two in the afternoon by the time we sat down at Gram and Pawpaw's long dining room table for Sunday Dinner, or what most people referred to as lunch. Sunday Dinner was another one of those "traditions" Gram was so keen on. It was like having Thanksgiving once a week: roast chicken (Pawpaw wasn't allowed fried anymore), ham, broccoli, green-bean casserole, biscuits, baked apples, spoon bread. If you named a dish with butter, bread, or bacon (or better yet, all three), it was on Belmont's table.

Their house was the one thing I actually loved about Beaufort. Belmont was all that was left of an old cotton plantation—in its time, a relatively modest estate that had been saved from demolition only by virtue of the fact that anything antebellum in the South is considered hallowed ground. The house stood on thirty acres of land at the back of what was now a subdivision of

McMansions called Lee's Landing—despite the fact General Lee never "landed" anywhere remotely nearby. There wasn't even a river.

With the exception of necessary restorations and modernizations, Belmont still looked much like it did in the brittle, yellowed photographs that hung in glass cases in its front hallway. There was a long, unpaved driveway, lined with ancient oak trees that grew together into a leafy, green canopy overhead. And while the house's white paint was peeling in places, and the second-story porch looked like it might collapse if it weren't for the four huge columns holding it up—when I was little, I used to try to wrap my arms around them; ever since we'd gotten here, I'd wanted to try again when no one was looking—it appeared like something out of a movie.

Inside, Gram "honored the house's past" by furnishing it with uncomfortable antiques on which Scarlett O'Hara herself could have reclined, but which felt like straw. And no matter how often it was cleaned, Belmont always smelled like dust. I'd once told my mother that it smelled like history. Truthfully, the house's past had terrified me as much as it had fascinated me. As a kid, I'd spent a good deal of time studying the faded photographs of my great-greats and great-great-greats on the walls. I knew most of them hadn't actually lived in the house (my great-grandfather bought it after the

Depression), but I'd still believed one of their ghosts might one day walk through a wall, carrying a musket for hunting Yankees, not unlike Elmer Fudd hunting "wabbit."

Every time I sat down to Sunday Dinner, these memories flooded my mind like the smell of frying fat flooded my senses. This Sunday was no exception; the cook had been busy. My mouth was watering, and if my grandfather didn't hurry up with the grace, I could not be held responsible for drooling. At his request, we bowed our heads.

"Bless, O Lord, this food to our use, and make us ever mindful of the needs of others. Amen. Ann Gordon, please pass the broccoli."

I had barely picked up my fork when Virginia piped up. "So, Annie, what's the deal with you and Robert Lee?" My cousin was staring at me intently from across the table, her chin propped on a Pink Passion–manicured hand.

"Virginia, please keep your elbows off the table," Gram scolded.

"Sorry, Gram." Virginia quickly put her hands in her lap, but the reprimand did nothing to break her laser-beam attention on me. "So do you like, know him? Are y'all dating?"

"No," I said defensively, cutting my eyes at her as I passed a plate of rice. "Where'd you hear that?"

"We saw him throw that football to you at the game yesterday," Charlotte drawled knowingly. It was like being interrogated by Tweedledee and Tweedledum.

"I mean"—I had to be very careful, as I knew no bit of potential gossip escaped these little rumormongers—"he's in one of my classes. We talk sometimes."

Virginia gasped like she might faint. "He's sooo cute! Are you gonna go out with him?" She spoke in a breathy rush.

"Virginia's like, totally in love with him," Charlotte said, plopping a biscuit on her plate.

"Our whole grade is, Charlotte, not just me." Virginia glared menacingly at her sister before turning her gaze back on me.

I could feel the blush creeping on. "Well, no! I barely know him, all right?"

"Maybe he could be an escort!" Charlotte exclaimed.

"Excuse me?" I asked, my knife poised in mid-air, ready to slather an extravagant slab of butter across my biscuit. In my experience, escorts were not a topic of conversation for polite society. They belonged in the black-and-white ads in the back of magazines, next to bust-enhancement pills. . . . Not that I ever read them.

"You have to invite two guys to be your escorts for the Magnolia Ball," Charlotte explained condescendingly.

I tensed. It aggravated the living bejeezus out of me when they did this, talking to me like I was some clueless foreigner and they were my patient guides to All Things Southern. If I had wanted their guidance, I'd have asked.

Aunt Nonny, who always "couldn't help but over-hear," took the opportunity to jump in.

"Robert Lee? That's Sassy Lee's son. Oh, he's quite the catch, Annie! He's just adorable." She winked, then took a dainty bite of plain rice. Leave it to Aunt *Nonny* to know someone named Sassy.

"Very good family," Gram added from her end of the table.

Wonderful, I thought—let's get the whole family's opinion on my nonexistent relationship with a boy I barely know. Next up, frank discussions with my grand-father about sex!

"It was such a shame when his father passed away last year," said Aunt Nonny.

My heart skipped a beat. I hadn't heard anything about Robert's father. Of course, I guessed that wasn't the sort of thing one went around advertising, especially to relative strangers.

"He is an attractive boy, isn't he?" Gram contin-ued. Apparently death wasn't enough to get her off topic. "He was the boy escorting Rowland Farley's grand-daughter last year, Gordon."

Pawpaw nodded. "Ah, yes, nice boy," he dutifully concurred, not looking up from his plate.

"Well, I'm not looking to 'catch' anyone, and I don't really see myself debbing, so . . ." I shoveled a fork of spoon bread into my mouth, hoping to put a definitive end to this unwanted conversation.

Suddenly I got the feeling I'd said something terribly gauche. It was like one of those scenes in the old Westerns, where the town is silent with dread and a lone tumbleweed rolls across the screen. I looked up to find Virginia and Charlotte staring at me dumbfounded, as if I'd slapped them. Aunt Nonny had a strange, thin smile frozen on her face and a quizzical look in her eye.

"One doesn't *see* oneself debbing, Ann Gordon. One just does," Gram pronounced.

Cue tumbleweed. Gram was always proper, definitely bossy, and not exactly warm, but tonight her voice had an hard edge I'd never heard before, not even after the disastrous Junior League luncheon. I swallowed my spoon bread, which I had in my momentary shock stopped chewing, and looked to my dad. He gave me a tiny, reassuring shake of his head.

Even poor Uncle Tripp thought he might come to my rescue. "Gordon," he said, diving in headfirst, "you'll never guess who I saw th'other weekend. I was down in 'lanta for business, and, of all people, I ran into Sally Miller—well, now Sally Gray, I s'pose. Hadn't seen her in ages, since y'all were an item back in college. You 'member?"

Whatever air had been left in the room after my big announcement was now completely sucked out.

"Of course he remembers her, Tripp. They were almost married," Gram snapped. "You know, after you moved up North, Gordon, she stayed in Atlanta. Met the nicest man from Savannah. I saw her mother the other day at the club. They have three sons."

"Wow, that's great," my dad said, with obviously forced enthusiasm. I knew he hated when Gram did this, brought up the old "girl who got away" in front of my mom.

Even I knew the story by now. My father met Sally in college. They'd "gone together" while he was living in Atlanta and working for a law firm, before he changed his mind and abandoned law for academia and Sally for Brown, my mom, and the dreaded North.

"She was a nice girl. You know, I was upset when it didn't work out," Gram continued, either not getting Dad's hint that he didn't want to talk about it or just not caring. I couldn't help but take the swipe at my mother personally. Different wife = different mother = different granddaughter.

My father's rosy complexion was steadily deepening. "Well, water under the bridge now. Judith, would you like this last biscuit?" he asked diplomatically.

"No thanks, hon. I'm fine," my mom answered. My mother never said much at these dinners. She liked to sit at the end and talk with Pawpaw, which worked out well, since she was the only one who would listen to his war stories over and over—and over, again.

Even Aunt Nonny could see this conversation was heading nowhere good and nervously tried to steer it to safer ground. "Mother, what did you think of the sermon this morning? Reverend Clarke's so young, I worried at first he wouldn't be able to handle St. John's."

"Well, our last priest was a bit too hellfire-and-brimstone for me," said Gram, resting her knife and fork on the side of her plate. For a moment, it looked as if Aunt Nonny had miraculously pulled through. "I think Reverend Clarke's more accessible. I hear he gets on well with the youth congregation."

Then she turned to me. Oh no, no, I was not off the hook yet.

"Ann Gordon, that's one thing that bothered me about your growing up all the way up there. Your father never gave you Church."

"Mother, we've talked about this." My father was losing his patience. "Judith is Jewish, and we *both* decided we'd let Annie make her own religious choices when she was old enough to make an informed decision."

"Well, I don't see why she couldn't have gone to church *and* celebrated Hanukkah." Gram gave her son a steely look. "Jesus was a Jew."

My father finally exploded. "Mother, do you know

how anti-Semitic you sound right now?" Gripping the table until his knuckles were white, it looked as if he were trying to keep from hurdling out of his seat and throttling his mother in a roomful of witnesses.

"Gordon, I resent that! I am *not* prejudiced! Judith knows I have great respect for her people."

"Respect for her *people*?" he repeated, shaking his head. I could almost swear, his eyes flashed red. "Sure you do. Enough to let them handle your money, but not to let them into your clubs, right?" he muttered under his breath.

My eyes widened. Oh shit! Maybe Gram hadn't heard.

But Pawpaw had. He snapped alive. "That's enough, Gordon. You don't speak to your mother that way."

"Gordon, let's not get into this," my mom said, pale and tight-lipped. "I hardly think your mother is anti-Semitic. She has a valid point; there are lots of people who raise their kids in both traditions. Our thing, Mary," she said, calmly turning to Gram and repeating something I knew she'd already explained to my grandmother at least a thousand times before, "was that we didn't want to force *any* religion on Annie. We want her to come to it on her own, if she feels it."

"Thank you, Judith. I appreciate your opinion, and if I've learned anything, it's that there's more than one way to raise a child. Who am I to judge?" Gram said, the irony escaping her.

With that, she carefully placed her folded napkin on the table. The conversation was officially over.

"Girls, will you please clear the table for dessert?"

For the first, and possibly last, time in our lives, Virginia, Charlotte, and I shared the same thought. We sprang from our chairs and fled to the kitchen like refugees from a civil war zone.

"I can't believe you're mad at me for sticking up for you," my father grumbled as he pulled the seat belt across his lap later that afternoon.

"I don't *need* you to stick up for me, Gordon," my mother said. "I'm perfectly capable of doing it myself. I've been dealing with your mother for twenty years."

I silently spun my turquoise ring in the backseat and pretended I couldn't hear my parents fighting, as if there were a soundproof plate of glass between us, like the taxis in New York.

"Fine, then I'll leave you to your own devices," he said as he steered the Volvo down the driveway in a cloud of dust.

"That's right. You're good at that, leaving me to my own devices." My mother laughed, but it wasn't a funny, ha-ha laugh; it was a pissed-off laugh that kind of scared me.

"What is that supposed to mean, Judith?" My father was starting to raise his voice. He never raised his voice.

Now it appeared he was going to do it twice in one day.

"Gordon, do you have any idea how hard this move has been on me? It's not exactly easy for an artsy, Yankee, Jewish woman to make friends with Bitsy and Bitty and Maddy and Taddy. For some God-knows-why reason, all these women have the most idiotic names. Someone tried to call me *Judy* the other day, Gordon. I am *not* a Judy!"

My mother was freaking out, but I kind of agreed with her. Yeah, what she said, I thought, but didn't dare weigh in.

Gazing straight ahead, with both hands firmly on the steering wheel, my father kept silent. I knew he was counting to ten.

"I'm sorry, Judith," he finally said, calm again. "I didn't know you were feeling that way. I guess I have been escaping into my work a little. There's so much to be done. . . . Believe me, it's strange for me to be back, too, but it must be even harder for you and Annie."

"That's another thing, Gordon. I don't like all this pressure on Annie about a debut." My mother made a mocking, exaggerated wave of her hand. "It's been tough on her as it is, making all these adjustments."

"All right, I'll talk to Mother," he deferred.

"And tell her to stop rubbing our noses in the education fund, too."

"*All right*, Judith. I said I'd talk to her."

I was way past uncomfortable now. The invisible glass was not there, and this all sounded too serious. No one wants to hear her parents fight, especially when it's about her.

When we got home later, I went straight for my room. Grabbing my cell phone off the cluttered desk, I plunked down on the floor and dialed Jamie's number. Straight to voice mail.

Sighing, I hung up the phone and stared up at Bob. Apparently the only lifeline I had left to the "normal" world was out actually *having* a life. Oh, the irony.

EIGHT

A lady promptly accepts or declines an invitation.

The 7-Eleven was teeming with middle schoolers. Two boys chased each other through the parking lot as a tight circle of skinny girls collapsed in exaggerated hysterics, their gaping mouths dyed an alarming red from their gallon-size Slurpees.

After hockey practice, the Marys had asked if I wanted to grab a Slurpee. To my own surprise, I had agreed. Which meant I now found myself precariously perched on the edge of my seat, searching for a way to sit so that my sweaty, mud-flecked legs wouldn't dirty the leather of Mary Katherine's very new-smelling SUV. A country song about placing bets on "Nashvegas" blared from the Bose speakers as she jerked the car into a parking spot.

"Ugh, obnoxious," MK hissed a minute later when a boy almost knocked her over as we stepped into the fluorescent lighting of the convenience store. "My brother's that age," she explained, heading to the candy aisle. "Okay, what I really want is a MoonPie, but should I be good and go for the Twizzlers instead?"

"That depends. What's a MoonPie?" I asked.

Mary Katherine gasped and put her hands on her tiny hips. "Only the sweetest little bit of prepackaged heaven you'll ever put in your mouth! You've seriously never had one?"

"Um, no. Not so big in Connecticut."

"Well, today's your lucky day, my friend." She plucked a plastic-wrapped, chocolate-covered, marshmallowy cookie-looking thing off the shelf and tossed it at me.

"So, MK, what happened to eating healthy?" Mary Price came up behind us.

"Diet starts tomorrow," Mary Katherine replied over her shoulder as she joined the back of the line at the Slurpee machine.

"I'm just gonna grab a soda," I said, heading for the refrigerator case, my cleats click-clacking on the yellow linoleum floor.

"A *soda*?" Mary Price repeated in a grating accent.

"First of all, that was a Minnesota accent." I laughed. "And yeah, a soda—like a Coke."

"It's just *Coke*."

"But what if I don't want a Coke? What if I want a Sprite or a root beer or something?"

"Nope. Coke. Always just *Coke*. Like referring to all tissues as *Kleenex*."

"Well, at least I don't say *pop*," I said, grabbing a Diet Coke out of the refrigerator case.

With Slurpees and "Coke" in hand, we sped down Azalea Avenue toward my house. Mary Katherine's driving skills suggested she might be a hazard to society. It usually made me nervous when people drove fast, but at the moment I was laughing too hard to notice. Mary Price was in the middle of an animated account of how she had accidentally seen her brother's college roommate "nekkid."

"Y'all, I swear, I thought I was gonna faint. I didn't know they could get that big. It was like elephantitis or something."

Tears were literally rolling down my cheeks. Between gasps, I asked how Mary Price had managed the full frontal to begin with.

"He was fixin' to get in the shower, and I guess he left the door open."

"He was fixing the shower *naked*?" I howled.

Mary Price laughed harder. "No! He was fixin' to take a shower."

I didn't get it.

"He was getting ready to get in the shower," she explained, catching my confused look in the rearview mirror.

"Ohhh." I nodded slowly. I was still giggling, but the

moment had been lost in translation.

"Cute," Mary Katherine said, as we pulled up to my house. Grabbing my backpack, stick, and gym bag, I thanked them and hurried from the car. I was aware that our house, no matter how "cute," probably looked like a shed compared to the massive villas and mansions in Lee's Landing, where the Marys probably lived. I thanked them for the ride.

"No problem," said Mary Katherine, popping her gum and dangling her thin, sun-freckled arm out the front window.

"See ya tomorrow," Mary Price called as I unlocked the door.

The silence in the front hall told me no one was home. I dumped my things by the door and went to the kitchen to throw my empty "Coke" in the recycling bin, chuckling again at Mary Price's story.

On the faux marble counter was a neat stack of mail and a single, business-size envelope set apart from the rest. I glanced at the return address. It was from the student-athlete scholarship fund. Immediately my heart raced and all lingering traces of laughter died. Without pausing, I tore open the envelope and read: "Dear Miss MacRae, After great deliberation, we regret to inform you . . ."

I hadn't gotten the scholarship. My head swam as I tried to make sense of the words on the page. "We *regret*

to inform you"? What did that mean? After great deliberation, you regret to inform me that you've thrown me to
the wolves? You regret to inform me that you've put me
at the mercy of my grandmother? I crunched the letter
in my fist and hurled it in the trash. Propping my elbows
on the countertop, I cradled my head in my hands.

Which was when I saw the *other* envelope. This one
was larger and square, edging out from the pile. I picked
it up. It was heavy, the cream-colored paper thick and
expensive-feeling. My name and address were elegantly
handwritten; I could see where the calligrapher's pen
had touched down. The return address was embossed
on the back: Beaufort Heritage Society.

Warily this time, I slid my finger under the envelope's
flap, with a premonition that whatever was inside would
not agree with me. As I pulled the invitation from the
envelope, a square of tissue paper dropped to the floor.
My jaw followed.

You are cordially invited
by the Beaufort Alabama Heritage Society
to make your debut at the
Magnolia Ball
Saturday evening, the twelfth of July
The Beaufort Country Club

Had I missed something? Because I had never agreed

to this. In fact, I *thought* I had made it perfectly clear that I would be a debutante only over my dead, blue, Yankee body.

The jarring ring of our telephone interrupted my post-traumatic shock. Still staring at the invitation, I picked up the handset and punched TALK.

"Hello?"

"Is this the MacRae residence?" the familiar voice on the other end asked. My blood boiled.

"Yes, it is." *You know damn right it is.*

"Then you should answer that way, Ann Gordon," said Gram.

Glaring at our refrigerator for lack of a better target, I twisted my turquoise ring furiously. "Hello, Gram, this is the MacRae residence. Dad's not here."

Gram either missed, or ignored, my sarcasm. "Well, that's fine because I was calling for you. The season will be starting soon, and I want to make sure you've received your invitation from the Heritage Society."

For God's sake, did the woman have a video camera trained on our house?! Grimacing, I answered yes.

"Wundaful," Gram said cheerfully. "You do know you need to respond with a handwritten note as soon as possible, don't you?"

"No, I did not know that," I said through clenched teeth.

"Congratulations, Ann Gordon," Gram said with not

even a hint of the irony I found in that statement. "This is quite an honor." She waited for me to say thank you, and when I didn't, she continued pleasantly. "Please let your father know I called. We have details to discuss."

"I'll do that," I said. Believe me, I'll do that, I thought, wondering how long my father had known this letter was on its way.

I said good-bye and punched the OFF button with such force I thought I might have broken the phone. No scholarship *and* a debutante ambush on the same day. It was a sick cosmic joke.

Turning the heavy envelope over in my hands again, I stared at my name in calligraphy. The curlicues and flourishes mocked me. But there was something missing. A stamp. The invitation had been hand delivered. Gram was making sure I got the message. She needn't have worried. I had gotten it . . . loud and clear.

"Hello?" my mom's voice called, followed by the sound of keys clinking in the ceramic dish in the front hall.

"In here," I replied glumly.

I didn't know how long I'd been sitting at the kitchen table, staring at the invitation, and coming up with Plans B through Z: a job, the lottery, selling my cousins on eBay. There had to be a way to pay for Brown without becoming—shudder—a deb.

My mother was surprised to find me in the kitchen.

The light outside had faded, and it was almost dark. She flipped on the overhead light and reached for a glass from the cabinet. "How was your day?"

"I think we need to have a little chat," I said by way of an answer. It was the same tone she used with me when I was about to get grounded.

She didn't speak right away but instead turned on the faucet, filling her glass and collecting her words before turning to me. "I saw the letter from the scholarship fund. . . ." she started, attempting to sound positive.

"Yeah, I didn't get it," I fired, quickly dispensing with that part of the day's good news. "But I did get this." I held up the envelope from the Heritage Society.

Her expression swiftly morphed from hope to sympathy to what I thought might be regret. "Annie, I know you're upset," she started, taking a seat at the table. "We meant to talk to you about it earlier."

"You *knew* what Gram was plotting, and you didn't tell me? You *knew* this was a sure thing?" So much for a controlled voice—I was almost yelling.

"Annie, before you get bent out of shape," my mother said sternly, "let me tell you about the conversation your father had with your grandmother."

I crossed my arms defiantly, protectively.

"Annie, Gram brought the deb issue up again with your dad a few days ago, when they were discussing college. As you know, your grandparents will be paying for most of it. We wish it weren't that way"—my mother closed her eyes and shook her head—"but it is. Gram is a very traditional woman, Annie." Her eyes were pleading. "She is happy to pay for your education—and we're lucky that she can—but Gram expects you to do this for her in return."

"Those were her exact words?" I was incredulous.

"No," she sighed. "Her exact words were, 'I will not pay for an education that does not include a lesson in being a lady.'"

"So she's bribing me? That's insane!" I was definitely yelling now. "That's not kind-hearted generosity, that's manipulation!"

"I know, Annie. Trust me, I know," she said softly. "But that's the way Gram is. This is very important to her, and you're her only chance because Uncle Tripp's not in the Heritage Society."

"Why doesn't she pressure Aunt Nonny to divorce him and marry someone who is, then?" I asked bitterly.

"Annie," my mother said firmly, "this really doesn't have to be such a big deal. I know it seems old-fashioned and stupid to you—to be honest, I agree with you—but it's not like she's asking you to shave your head and join the circus. It's a few parties, really. And it's worth it, if that will make her happy and you'll get the money you need for college."

"I can't believe you're saying this!" I jumped up from my chair, practically hysterical, and began pacing our small kitchen like a tiger in a cage. "You're such a traitor! You know this isn't me. This isn't who I am!"

"Annie, she's not asking you to change who you are."

"Yes, Mom, she is." Tears were stinging my eyes. "She always has."

The tears must have triggered some parental feeling of guilt, because my mother suddenly looked sad. "Annie, when your father moved away to go back to school, Gram disagreed with his decision. She cut him off financially, and he had to pay his own way. It wasn't easy. I know it's hard to think about now, but debt is not something you want to burden yourself with this young."

"I'll work. Maybe McDonald's is hiring," I argued half seriously.

"Annie, please take my word on this. Brown is well worth making your debut for Gram. Besides, Gram is getting older. I know better than anyone that she can be manipulative—"

"Which is why you, of all people, should have stood up for me!" I interrupted.

"—but she's not going to be around forever." She tried to take my hand, but I pulled away. "Annie, she loves you very much, and in her own way, she actually thinks she has your best interest at heart."

I was silent, letting the betrayal hang heavy in the air between us. "I thought at least *you'd* understand," I hissed.

Hoping that the depth of my disappointment had been conveyed in that final sentence, I pounded up the stairs to my room.

At one that morning, I was still wide awake, staring at the moon-streaked ceiling from my wet pillow. My eyes were puffy and my nose was stopped up. If only Gram could have seen me—the portrait of a lady.

For two hours I'd alternated between beating my fists into the pillow and rocking back and forth in sobs of self-pity. And Jamie, the only person I could talk to, was asleep—happily—in her comfortable Connecticut bed.

What was I going to do? I wanted to stand up to Gram, tell her she could take her "season" and shove it, that I couldn't be bought. But I also wanted to go to Brown and get out of this stupid fishbowl of a town.

Finally exhausted, I made my decision. I'd play Southern Belle Barbie if that's what Gram wanted. But play is all it would be. She could put the girl in the debutante, but not the debutante in the girl.

NINE

*A lady knows when an evening
has come to its end.*

My butt was going numb on the stone bench outside the language building as I finished *The Sound and the Fury* for Mr. Smith. It was getting cold, or at least what qualified as cold in Alabama, and I pulled my purple hoodie around me tightly. Oddly, I was happy for the distraction school was providing from the deb situation.

Hearing the crunch of footsteps in the fallen leaves, I looked up to find Robert Lee loping toward me with a playful smile. Not for the first time, it occurred to me that my cousins might be justified in their little crush. He was cute with his flannel shirt coming untucked from his khakis and his curls sticking out from under the perfectly curved brim of his hat.

"Hey," he said, striding up to the bench. "This seat taken?"

"No." I closed my dog-eared book and tried to assume a casual posture as he sat down.

"What's up?" he asked when he was settled.

He sat the way men do, with his legs splayed, leaning forward to rest his forearms on his knees, so that he had to turn his head to see me.

"Not much. Catching up on reading for English."

"Yeah, I probably should have started that," he drawled.

"Probably." I grinned and wondered if he really hadn't, or if he was just trying to impress me. Which made me wonder why I cared. Snapping myself out of it, I added, "Mr. Smith's such a jerk it kind of scares me into doing the reading. Maybe that's his teaching philosophy."

Robert laughed. "Missed you at the game last weekend. Last one of the season!" His tone implied this might be an offense punishable by stoning.

"I skipped it," I confessed. "I have to admit I'm not much of a football person."

He feigned shock. "Not a football person? You *are* in Alabama now. You do know that, right? Them er fightin' words 'round here," he warned, exaggerating his accent for effect.

Now it was my turn to laugh. "So I hear."

"What are you up to tonight?" He straightened so we were now eye level.

My stomach fluttered nervously. "Um, I don't know. Not much, probably," I finally answered.

"Bliss's parents are out of town for the weekend. She's having people over. You wanna come?"

I fidgeted with the place where my ring usually was. Accidentally I had left it on my dresser that morning, which was proving quite unhelpful in a situation like this.

"Um, yeah, that'd be fun . . . but I don't really have a car," I added quickly.

Robert laughed and looked at me like I wasn't catching his drift. Wow, I thought, his eyelashes are *really* long.

"Well, I was kind of thinkin' I could pick you up and take you. . . ."

"Oh! Uh," I stammered. "Um, that's really nice of you. That would be fun, but I think I may have to hang out with my parents."

I was giving myself an out, although I wasn't totally sure why. It didn't occur to me that I might *actually* go with him.

"My dad's all excited. He's cooking dinner, and it's this big deal 'cause he never cooks . . . and he Netflixed this movie I've been dying to see. . . ." I was rambling. I did that when I lied through my teeth.

"Don't want to disappoint your dad," Robert said, seeming a little disappointed himself. I followed his gaze to his hands. They looked strong, with long, thin fingers. He stood abruptly and gave me another smile. "Offer stands if you change your mind. See ya in class."

I watched him as he strode quickly away. Damn it! *I'm hanging out with my parents?* What? That was about as cool as saying, "Sorry, dude, updating my *Lord of the Rings* blog tonight." Why had I turned him down? In all fairness, I had been nervous. And it was unexpected. But he was cute and asking me out, and, let's face it, I hadn't had too many offers lately. . . . Should I really go? I couldn't spend another Friday night at home. . . . But I'd just turned him down!

I needed backup assistance. Country Day had a strict no cell phones policy, but this qualified as an emergency. I discreetly pulled my phone from my backpack and speed-dialed Jamie's number. Lucky girl had the day off; it was Deerwood's parent-teacher conference day.

One ring . . . two . . . three . . .

"Annie! Hey. What's up?" When she finally answered, Jamie's voice on the other end sounded startled and staccato.

"Hey. I need your advice. There's a guy here who's kinda cute—and sweet, but *so* not my type—well, maybe a *little* my type . . . Wait, where are you?" There was loud traffic in the background, and laughter.

"In the City. We're in line for tickets to the Panic show. You should see this line. We've been sitting on the sidewalk for like, three hours!"

"Who's there?" I asked.

"Umm, Bodie, Jake, me, and Beth."

I knew Beth and Bodie had been hooking up, but wait, had she said . . . "Jake?"

"Yeah," she replied, with that very subtle raising of the voice that *implied* innocence.

"Why is *he* there?" My stomach turned inside out. Mental check: Jamie was my best friend. Jake was my cheating ex-boyfriend. According to all codes of friendship, they should not be snuggling up in line together for what sounded a whole lot like a double date.

Suddenly it clicked, more than a click, more along the lines of a lightning bolt: *That's* why Jamie had been so insistent about not wasting my time missing Jake, telling me to move on. *That's* why she had been taking forever to e-mail back and texting instead of returning my calls. Jamie was hooking up with Jake! I'd been gone for three months and my best friend and ex-boyfriend . . . I shook my head and squinched my eyes to shut out the thought.

"Jamie, is there something you need to tell me?" There was a tidal wave of nausea rising in my throat. I put my head between my legs and told myself that I couldn't cry, not here.

"No," she replied tentatively. I was quiet. Her lie stung. "Yes," she exhaled.

"Oh my God."

"Annie, I've been meaning to talk to you about it for a while. . . ."

"Oh my God," I repeated.

"Now's not really a good time . . ."

"Yeah, no kidding." I clapped the phone shut as the bell rang inside the language building, a painful reminder that while my world was crashing down around me, life, seemingly, went on.

I barely registered a word Mr. Smith said in English. My notes looked like the disjointed diary of a schizophrenic: "narrative voices," "symbolism," "fall from grace," "death=redemption?" In the middle of the page I had scrawled the word "betrayal." It stared back at me. Should I have seen it coming?

When the last bell rang, I made sure I was the first person out of the room. Robert followed with Smalley, laughing about some joke he'd made during class that I myself had only half heard through my jumbled thoughts. One thing was clear, though—I had changed my mind.

"Hey, Robert?" I hoped I sounded more confident than I felt. I also really wished Smalley wasn't standing there.

Robert looked up, surprised to see me waiting for him.

"I was just wondering if the offer still stands tonight? I mean about the party." Did I sound as pathetic as I did in my head?

"What happened to date-night with the parents?" he teased.

"I'm two-timing them." I had meant it to sound light-hearted, but the shadow of Jamie and Jake crossed my mind, and instead it came out with a sharp, cynical edge that I then tried to cover with an awkward laugh.

Robert didn't seem to notice. "All right. I'll pick you up at eight, then?"

"Great. See you then."

Who needed those traitors anyway? Maybe it was time for some "Southern Comfort."

By the time my doorbell rang at precisely one minute past eight (give those Southern gentlemen a hand—at least they're punctual), half my closet was on my bed. After school, I'd cried as I tore clothes off hangers and discarded them onto the floor, mentally telling off both Jake and Jamie in a dozen different ways that involved expletives I hadn't even known were in my arsenal.

The more pressing issue before me, however, was what to wear. Did people here dress up to go out? Or down? I'd finally settled on jeans and a blue shirt I'd been told made my eyes "pop." And, after deciding my first attempt at makeup resembled a prostitute from *Moulin Rouge* (I'd never really gotten the makeup thing—part of the reason my usual routine consisted of cover-up and Chap Stick), I'd washed it all off and started over again.

As I came down the stairs, my father and Robert appeared gradually, from the feet up. Weird. My dad had never chatted up Jake before we went out. On second thought, I guess I'd always met Jake out; he never picked me up. Yet another sign of his despicable ways, his backstabbing, cruel, horrible, vile . . . I forced my thoughts back to the situation at hand as Robert and my father's conversation filtered in.

"Yes, sir. I'm thinkin' either Chapel Hill or Virginia," Robert said. His hands were stuffed in his khaki pockets. He looked cleaned up. For me? I wondered.

"Chapel Hill? I went there for undergrad. Of course, that was eons ago." My father rocked back and forth on his feet, chuckling like what he'd said was even remotely funny. "Good school. Let me know if I can be of help."

"Thank you, sir. I 'preciate it."

When I reached the landing on the stairs, they both looked up. This was awkward.

"Pitching your alma mater, Dad?"

"Yep, Robert here"—my father slapped him lightly on the back—"was just telling me he's applying to Carolina."

"That's great, Dad. Well"—I turned to Robert—"ready to go?"

"Sure."

I headed for the door, but Robert lingered back a second with my father.

"Nice to meet you, Mr. MacRae."

"Nice to meet you too, son. Y'all have a good time, and Annie, remember curfew's twelve thirty."

What? Jake was never "son." And the "sir" stuff? All this chivalry crap was strange, I thought, until Robert walked to the passenger side of his rusty, red Bronco and opened the door for me. Then it was kind of nice.

In fact, I was impressed—until we pulled into the Dairy Queen. Weren't we supposed to be going to a party? Sudden Blizzard craving? But instead of pulling into one of the parking spaces in front, Robert circled to the back of the building, where four cars were already parked and a dozen kids I recognized from school were milling around in the pool of headlights.

"What's this?" I asked.

"We usually caravan to parties. Not sure why, really. I guess no one likes to show up alone." He shrugged.

"Hey, ladies," he called as he swung his car next to Smalley's pickup. "Are we goin' to this party, or what?"

Mary Katherine was leaning on the far side of Smalley's car, her head stuck through the open passenger window. "Robert, my dear," she said, "the party waits for no one. Let's go."

Then, noticing me in the passenger seat, she smiled. "Hey, Annie."

*   *   *

Bliss's house was massive and Mediterranean-style, with a tile roof and a large fountain in the middle of a circular driveway that was already crowded with an assortment of expensive SUVs.

Again, Robert opened my door before grabbing a case of Pabst Blue Ribbon from the trunk. He guided me around the house to a side porch, where a small group was gathered around a glass table, playing a drinking game that involved flipping the emptied plastic cups onto the table. The table and ceramic floor beneath were already completely soaked with beer.

Robert's hand landing lightly on my waist sent a spark up my spine. It made me feel *just maybe* I could actually belong at a party in the middle of Alabama with a bunch of kids I barely knew—or at least I could pretend for one night. He led me through a sliding-glass door into a sunroom, which was like stepping into a layout from *Southern Living*. Everything that could be upholstered was covered in pastel florals. There were expensive-looking porcelain and glass knickknacks everywhere. Through the living room, I could see a larger-than-life oil painting of Bliss sitting demurely on a blanket under a tree.

Then I heard a sound I hadn't heard in months: coins bouncing off a hard countertop. As we came into the kitchen, a loud greeting rose from the boys crowded around the island counter. Correction—from all except Smalley—who was busy chugging a beer, a thin line of golden liquid dribbling down his chin and onto his red fleece.

"Hey, fellas," Robert said. "You know Annie, right?"

The guys chorused some polite, halfhearted hellos, but most were already absorbed again in the game of quarters.

"Ryker." Mary Katherine's boyfriend, good-looking with blond wings flying out from under an Alabama hat, nodded his head in introduction.

"Hey." I nodded in return. Of course I already knew who he was—he came to hockey games and sat with Robert and Smalley at lunch every day—but I tried to sound casual, like I might be noticing these people for the first time as well. Like I hadn't known who they were for the past *three* months.

Robert handed me a beer before sticking the case in the already full refrigerator.

"Aren't you gonna have one?" I asked.

"Yeah, I'll get one in a minute. I'm driving," he said, shrugging.

The beer was semiwarm. Popping it open, I took a swig. It was slightly skunky, like it had been sitting in the back of a car too long, but I drank it anyway. When in Rome . . .

Robert was quickly engrossed in the game. I took

a seat next to him on a tall barstool, having declined an invitation to join in—not that I was opposed or hadn't played before, but there was apparently a different set of rules down here (as with everything else), and I didn't want to embarrass myself by looking like a rookie. Instead I drank and watched, silently appreciating when Robert included me with a smile or a comment.

A few beers into it, I was starting to enjoy what felt like a strange new reality show: *Real Life: I'm a Good Ol' Boy*. There was a pleasant, tingly feeling creeping from my feet to my legs, and everyone seemed friendlier than they had a couple hours earlier. Mary Katherine had decided to brave the game. She was surprisingly creative with her trash-talking and would grin as she plunked the quarter into the now bacteria-infested cup and watched her unfortunate victim empty it down the hatch. It was fascinating to see her hold court over this unruly, increasingly drunk bunch.

Finally, at nature's calling, I gave up my observation post and headed for the bathroom. It was mauve, with a pink toile shower curtain, seashell-shaped soaps, and monogrammed hand towels. I smoothed my hair in the mirror and adjusted my shirt, laughing to myself at the typically Southern paradox: decorative beach accents hundreds of miles from coastline. When I opened the door, the Marys were in the hall.

"Heya! What's up?" said Mary Price, with the loud enthusiasm that comes from a couple of drinks.

"We're going outside to have a cigarette. Wanna come?" Mary Katherine asked in her raspy (now I knew why) voice.

"Oh, thanks. I don't smoke."

"I know. It's totally gross, but this is tobacco country. Whatdyagonna do?" asked Mary Katherine. "I'll quit in college."

"Yeah right," said Mary Price, rolling her eyes. "I don't smoke either, but Butthead here needs someone to keep her company. Just come sit with us," she said, intertwining her arm through mine and leading me through the porch, where Flip-cup was still going strong, and outside.

The three of us sat side by side on the stairs of the large, stone patio. Mary Katherine pulled a crumpled pack of cigarettes from her back pocket. Balancing one between her glossed lips, she lit it and took a drag. She turned to me as she exhaled into the air above my head. "So, you're here with Robert?"

I tried to gauge the tone of Mary Katherine's question: catty or curious? Curious, I decided. "Yeah, I guess. I mean, he brought me."

"That's cool." She nodded.

"Robert's a really sweet guy," Mary Price offered, unsolicited. "He's one of my faves."

"Yeah, he seems great." I realized I meant it.

"Hey, Annie," a new voice said. It was Bliss, who had come up behind us and plopped down on the step. "I saw you and Robert come in together." Her voice was much warmer than she must have been. Her hair was curled, and though it was almost cold enough for a sweater, she wore a tight black tank top. Yet, oddly, I was the one who felt underdressed.

"Wait," Mary Katherine said suddenly, stomping her cigarette out beneath her boot. "Didn't you mention something about a boyfriend in Connecticut?"

The reminder hurt like a bruise you forget is there until you hit it again. I had mentioned Jake to the girls a few times in hockey.

"*Ex*-boyfriend," I clarified. "About as *ex* as you can get, actually. I found out today he's hooking up with my best friend. Correction: *ex*-best friend."

Mary Price gasped. "Seriously? That is *so* wrong!"

"That sucks," Mary Katherine affirmed (as if I hadn't already come to that conclusion).

"Oh, honey." Bliss frowned and put her hand on my knee. "Are you okay?"

I nodded, my own hands pressed between my knees. "Yeah, I'll be okay. I'm still kind of in shock, I think." I was relieved to talk about it, even though the words made the pain more real.

"Well, good riddance," said Mary Katherine. "The

guy I dated before Ryker cheated on me. I say, *Next!*"
She waved her hand, like there was an invisible line of
suitors queued up behind me.

I forced a thin laugh. "Easier said than done."

"Yeah, we know," sighed Mary Price.

"Y'all playin' nice out here?" Robert sauntered down
the steps and stood in front of us. From this vantage
point, he looked taller. His khakis hung loosely from his
narrow hips, and I couldn't help but notice the broad-
ness of his shoulders beneath his shirt.

"Just telling Annie about the time we stole your
pants when we all went skinny-dipping at Smalley's lake
house," Mary Price said, poker-faced.

"Very funny. Hope you did me justice." He winked,
then turned to me. "Annie, I hate to do this, but I think
maybe we oughtta head outta here before Smalley real-
izes I'm not drunk and tries to make me shoot bourbon.
I told my mom I'd help her in the morning with the
yard, and it's already twelve," he said, glancing at his
watch.

"Okay." I was ready anyway. I'd already been tipsy,
and now I was upset from the reminder about Jake and
Jamie. "I'll see you guys later," I said, standing to go.

As Robert and I walked away, Mary Katherine yelled
"Next!" after us, and I heard Bliss giggle.

"What's that about?" Robert asked, glancing back at
the girls.

"Don't worry about it." But I smiled. It felt nice to finally have someone on *my* side.

"So only your grandmother calls you Ann Gordon?"

"Yeah. She's like, hard-core, old-school Southern. It's driving me freaking crazy. She's trying to make me into a lady or something."

The Bronco jerked as Robert shifted gears.

"So what are you now?" he teased.

"Not a lady, apparently! She's making me do this debutante thing. No offense, as this seems to be some life-altering rite of passage for girls down here, but I don't see the sense in paying a ton of money to get all dolled up in a white dress and have a big party. Aren't you supposed to save that for your wedding? I mean, the whole concept is just so insanely idiotic to me. . . . Sorry . . ." I looked at him, causing my laugh to catch nervously in my throat. Those eyelashes! I could see them silhouetted in the streetlights.

"No apologies necessary," he said with a small smile. "I was an escort last year. It was fun, but it seemed like a lot of work for the girl."

"Exactly! And it's not even like it's something I really want to do. I'm being forced into it by my grandmother, and my dad's so absorbed in his new job he isn't even around to fend the old lady off. I mean, I miss him. Even when he's with us, he's not totally *with* us. He's stressed all the time. . . ." Realizing I was oversharing again, I faded off.

I cracked my window, and a cold wind hit my face. It would be winter soon, but for now the smell of fall still lingered on the air. It made me miss Connecticut. Fall had always been my favorite season. It was beautiful at home, with trees like orange, red, and gold fireworks. There was a little of that here, but it wasn't the same. It would never be the same.

Robert was quiet. *Shit.* I remembered like an electric shock: Robert's father was dead. *Shit shit shit.* How could I be so insensitive?

"Anyway . . ." I said meekly, trying my best to melt into the seat.

"Yeah, I miss my dad, too," he said finally. We had coasted to a stoplight, and he was staring straight ahead into the darkness. "He died last year."

"I'm so sorry."

And I was. Here was this boy with kind eyes sitting so stone-faced and brave right next to me. I wanted to make it better. I wanted to bring his father back for him. I at least wanted to hug him and tell him it'd be okay.

"How'd he die?" I asked instead, trying to walk the fine line between showing concern and prying.

"Drunk driver."

The light turned green and the Bronco lurched forward.

"It must have been tough on you moving down here," Robert said, changing the subject and glancing over at me. "And, trust me, I know what you mean about pain-in-the-ass grandparents. My grandma won't leave us alone, bringing over all my dad's old 'memorabilia' she's collected over the years. I think she still has his first diaper."

"Really?" I laughed.

"Oh yeah. Photo albums, basketball trophies from the seventies, the tux from his senior prom . . . I'm tellin' you, it's ridiculous. Our attic is so filled with his old stuffed deer heads and hunting gear, it even creeps *me* out to go up there. And I hunt!

"She's trying to pressure me to go to Chapel Hill," Robert continued. "That's where my dad went. It'd be fun. I like the idea of following in his footsteps, but I kind of feel like I've already done that. So many Beaufort people go, it'd be like Country Day all over again."

As he finished speaking, we pulled up to the curb in front of my house. By this point, that nice tingly feeling in my feet had crept up my legs, and my knees felt like Jell-O. Was Robert just saying what I wanted to hear, or was he really this cool? Because he was starting to sound—and look—awfully irresistible.

He turned off the engine. "Well, thanks for letting me take you out tonight, *Ann Gordon*."

"Yeah. I had fun. Much better than date-night with the parents." I laughed nervously.

"Good."

As Robert put one hand on the back of my seat and one on the steering wheel, I realized he was coming in for a kiss, and the jelly feeling vanished. I freaked. Leaning away from him, I launched into the worst case of verbal diarrhea in human history: "Umm, Jake—I mean Robert! I'm sorry . . . It's just really bad timing . . . I don't know . . . It's so stupid, but I had this boyfriend—Jake—in Connecticut. We broke up when I moved, but I just found out he hooked up with my best friend Jamie . . . in Connecticut. Or she hooked up with him. Whatever. He's a total jerk, and I shouldn't care about him. But it's just brought up a lot of old feelings. . . . It's just not that easy, ya know . . . to just drop everything . . . I'm sorry. I didn't know if this was like, a date, or just a friend thing. . . ."

I was babbling. Bad. I could hear myself talking but had no idea what I was saying. The words were tumbling out of my mouth. Definitely oversharing. For a second, Robert looked at me with an irresistible combination of utter confusion and amusement, then he retreated to his seat.

"Okay," he said. "That's fine. We can just call it a friend thing." He smiled reassuringly.

"Okay," I said tentatively, already wishing I could stuff the words back in my mouth and just kiss him. "Sorry."

"Don't be sorry. I had fun."

"Good. Me too. Okay, I'm gonna go now."

In a flash I was out of the car and all but running for safety. I turned at the front door. Robert had waited to make sure I got in the house. He waved, and as he pulled away, I questioned my mental health. What had I just done?

I woke up at noon the next day to three missed calls, all from Jamie. She wanted to talk, to explain. Her first message said things weren't as bad as they sounded. I doubted that. By the second message, she was begging me to call her. In the third, she was crying. I didn't care. I'd been crying for months. She could cry until she died from dehydration, for all I cared.

For the first time I saw how selfish Jamie could be. Her "live and let live" attitude wasn't free-spirited and refreshing; it was a way to get what she wanted without being responsible for the fallout. For years I'd thought we were two peas in a pod, but now I wondered if Connecticut and a third-grade refusal to drink milk were where our similarities began and ended.

I knew one day, after extensive therapy, I might find it in my heart to forgive her; but for now I decided to delete the voice mails and her number from my phone. It was a symbolic gesture, as I'd known her number by heart for years, but it made me feel better. What was done was done.

I just hoped the same wasn't true for Robert. Considering the private tour of Crazyland I'd given him the previous evening, I wasn't feeling so optimistic. Clearly, there was only one thing to do: go downstairs and drown my sorrows in coffee ice cream and *The Price is Right*.

TEN

A lady is a gracious victor.

There was less than one minute left on the clock in the hockey game, and call me immodest, but the score was four to one thanks in large part to me. St. Bernard's would *not* be winning the last game of the season.

Play was stopped after an overzealous midfielder had desperately hacked at my stick. Big mistake. Scanning the field, I saw that Bess, our other forward, was open. I sent my free hit flying and cut sharply down and to the right. Pivoting, I lost my defender and made a beeline for the goal, where Bess met me with a perfect pass back. In a single glorious swing, I redirected the ball past the stunned goalie. Five–one. Thanks for coming, St. B's.

Everyone went crazy. The team threw down their sticks and jumped off the bench, rushing to a victorious mosh pit at center field. Arms linked around one another's shoulders, we jumped up and down.

In the midst of the fray, I looked to the bleachers

for my parents. They were there . . . and so was Robert. He and Ryker stood on the sidelines, their arms crossed over their chests, talking. When had they appeared? My stomach flipped, and not in a good way. I hadn't talked to Robert since Friday night, when I'd word-vomited all over him.

Mary Katherine snapped her fingers in front of my face. "*Hel-lo?* You still with us? Come on. We have to do lineup."

Always good sports, we shook hands with St. Bernard's, now a dismal picture of defeat in plaid kilts. Applebutt insisted that we stretch together while she gave an inspirational postseason recap, which we dutifully ignored. I, for one, was too busy wondering how to handle my first post-incident run-in with Robert to concentrate on plays and "team synergy."

When Applebutt finally let us go, the team scattered to friends and family still waiting on the sidelines. My father was beaming. It was the first full game he'd seen all season.

"Great game, Banannie!" He threw his arm around my sweaty shoulders and hugged me.

"Good job, hon," said my mom.

"Thanks. Look, I'm gonna grab a Slurpee with some of the girls." I wanted them out of there. It was nice they came and all—being supportive, blah, blah, blah—but if I was going to have to face Robert after last weekend's meltdown, I didn't want the added humiliation of my parents watching.

"Okay." My mom shrugged.

"Hey, champ. Are you comin' with?" Mary Price walked up shining her toothpaste-commercial smile at my parents. Somehow she looked as fresh as if she'd just stepped out of a massage and facial as opposed to an hour-long hockey game. Her rosy pink cheeks were the perfect setting for her matching dimples.

"Mom, Dad, this is Mary Price. Mary Price, these are my parents."

"Nice to meet you," Mary Price said, in her parent voice. (This wasn't the first time I'd noticed this strange phenomenon. Kids down here had one voice for each other and a parent voice for older people, kind of like Jekyll and Hyde. It was slightly higher, with far better enunciation.)

"Annie, isn't that the boy who took you out the other night? Robert?" my dad asked, squinting over at Robert and Ryker.

"I guess so," I said dismissively. "Mary Price, I can get a ride home with you, right?" The last thing I needed was my father cornering Robert to reminisce about his days at UNC.

"Sure."

"Great! So, see you guys at home." I lightly pushed my parents toward the parking lot.

"But . . ." my dad started.

"All right," my mom said, taking him by the arm. "Come on, Gordon. We'll see her at home." My father looked baffled but followed her.

Mary Price smiled at me quizzically. "What was that about?"

"*That* was a story for another time." I wasn't sure I was ready to invite Mary Price and the other girls into the most recent exhibit in Annie MacRae's Hall of Shame. Not just yet.

"Okay." Mary Price didn't press. "Let's grab Mary Katherine, then."

Of course, Mary Katherine was standing with Robert and Ryker. Not "of course" because Mary Katherine was dating Ryker and friends with Robert and that was the logical place for her to be standing, but "of course" because that's just how my life seemed to be going these days. I followed Mary Price, hoping I might somehow hide behind her thin frame. No luck. He saw me.

"Hey," said Robert.

"Hey." So we were back to monosyllables.

He kicked at the dirt, his hands in his pockets. "Good game."

"Thanks." I looked down at my dirty cleats.

"How'd you get so good at hockey?"

I felt my athletic glow deepen into what I was sure was an arresting shade of magenta. "I'm not that good."

"Well." He shrugged. "I guess all you really have to do is hit a ball and run after it."

My mouth fell open at the affront, causing Robert to laugh. "Relax, Miss MacRae, I was just joking."

"I was about to say . . ." I objected. "I'd like to see how far you could hit a ball!"

"All right." He reached for my hockey stick.

I handed it to him and cocked my eyebrow. "Show us whatcha got, Bubba."

Robert trotted out to the field, where my winning ball was still lodged in the goal. Ryker, always up for a challenge, grabbed Mary Katherine's stick and took off after him. We laughed as the boys swung our sticks around like golf clubs.

"FORE!" Ryker yelled. He took a giant, arcing swing at the fluorescent hockey ball, missing it, and instead sending a sizable chunk of grass flying at Robert, who had to duck to avoid the spray of dirt.

"Nice, guys!" Mary Katherine yelled sarcastically onto the field, at which point Robert turned and shot me a mischievous grin. I returned it, which caused Mary Price to deliver a playful nudge to my ribs.

But she didn't know the half of it. There was some major relief behind my smile. Robert and I were okay. Or as okay as two people can be after one of them word vomits on the other.

As Ryker swung again, Mary Katherine heaved a

sigh. "Slurpee?" she asked without looking at us.

"Yes, please," Mary Price and I answered at the same time.

"Jinx," said Mary Price. "You owe me a Coke."

"You mean a soda?"

"You can call it whatever you want," she replied, slinging her gym bag over her shoulder, "but you still owe me one."

ELEVEN

If a lady has nothing nice to say, she says nothing at all.

"So it is with great pleasure and without further ado, that I introduce the chairwoman of this year's Magnolia Ball, Totty Patterson." Charles Manley, the president of the Beaufort Heritage Society—a distinguished, grandfatherly man in a gray suit and red bow tie—graciously yielded the podium to Mrs. Patterson, whom I so fondly remembered from the Junior League luncheon.

'Twas the season—the deb season—but I had no reason to be jolly. The Christmas Tea was the kickoff event at which the year's "chosen" were informed what the next seven months of our lives would look like. Of course I had been late, arriving just as Mr. Manley was taking the podium. My place card ("Miss Ann Gordon MacRae") was near the back, at a table with Mary Price and Taylor. I had been relieved to learn that the Marys were debutantes as well. I should have suspected, but nevertheless, it meant I would at least suffer with company. As I took my place between Mary Price and Taylor, I scanned the room. Mary Katherine was at the table next to us, along with my cheery neighbor Courtney. Conspicuously absent was Bliss.

Sequins on the embroidered snowflakes of Mrs. Patterson's Christmas theme–sweater twinkled in the soft, overhead light of the Heritage Society dining room. She beamed at the group of eager, bright-eyed young girls who, come July, would be introduced to Beaufort not just as women but, more important, as *ladies*.

Looking around the lavish dining room, with its brocade curtains and roaring fire in the marble fireplace, I tried to see my fellow debutantes as Totty Patterson must have: the cream of the crop, the best and brightest of Beaufort's progeny. Overwhelmingly, they were blond, thin, and attractive, with the exception of a handful who filled only a couple of those criteria. Expectantly, politely, they had turned their faces to gaze upon the woman who would guide them to be all they could be.

"First and foremost, a debutante is a lady," Mrs. Patterson began with such earnestness, such conviction, such sincerity, that it was hard for me to keep from laughing. I could just imagine Totty, hair in curlers, cold cream smeared across her round face, practicing this speech over and over in her bathroom mirror.

"As Mr. Manley so kindly reminds us, the Magnolia Ball is an important part of this city's rich history and one of Beaufort's most cherished traditions. While it no longer serves its historical purpose—" She paused, allowing space for a prim but conspiratorial smile to flicker across her face and a twitter to pass through the room. "It remains with us as a celebration of the entrance into adult society of our community's young leaders. While some might consider the season demanding—Beaufort does pride itself on a relatively lengthy and involved preparation—it readies you to enter that society with the grace and poise expected of a young lady.

"There will be lots of parties," she went on, looking from girl to girl. "That is one of the most exciting things about making your debut. After all, it is a celebration. But this is not just one big party, girls. You *must* remember that the Magnolia Ball is a charity event, one of Beaufort's longest running, and proceeds will go to Grace Children's Hospital. I have spoken with members of their board, and they are expecting the best ball yet."

Mrs. Patterson was gripping the heavy, wooden podium and speaking deliberately, as if to give her words weight and impress upon us that we would be dogooders, not princesses. The performance was too much for me.

"Saving the world one curtsy at a time," I quipped under my breath as I blew the steam from my cup of Earl Grey.

I hadn't meant for the comment to be heard, but Mary Price smiled and shot me a sideways glance. "Think not what the deb can do for you, but what you can do for the deb," she joked, to my surprise.

Since learning we were all in the deb together, I'd avoided talking about it with Mary Price and the other girls, assuming they would view this day with the same solemnity with which Totty did. For the first time, it occurred to me maybe I wasn't alone in my misery.

Mrs. Patterson's second-in-command was going table to table, passing out large manila packets that some of the girls ripped open ravenously. On top of the stack of papers inside—a phone tree, a list of dos and don'ts, literature on the Children's Hospital—was a three-page schedule of events on Heritage Society letterhead.

"Whoa," Mary Price said as she flipped through the schedule. Taylor shushed her, but Mary Price just frowned at her and then giggled.

I, on the other hand, was not yet capable of laughter, as I was too busy trying to get my eyes back into their sockets after seeing what was in store for the third week of January: ETIQUETTE I, 1–3 P.M., BEAUFORT WOMEN'S CLUB. Etiquette II was the following weekend. A brunch, tea, or lunch every month. A group community service outing to the hospital in April: 11 A.M.–1 P.M., VISIT WITH PATIENTS; 1–2 P.M., LUNCH WITH HOSPITAL BOARD. This event was emphasized with an asterisk and a note that photographers from *The Beaufort Bugle* would be invited. *So look cute, or else*, I read between the lines.

The entire week before the Magnolia Ball was blocked off. There were three dance rehearsals and one "figure rehearsal." I had no idea what a figure rehearsal entailed, but apparently it would take four hours out of my Thursday. Another note at the bottom of the last page warned us in menacing, bold print that tardiness would not be tolerated, and absence from more than one event would warrant dismissal from the debutante court. My heart sank. Apparently, my soul *and* the better part of my senior year had been sold to the debutante committee. Gloomily, I looked back to Mrs. Patterson.

"Now, I know what y'all have been waiting for. And let me precede this with a reminder that it is much more exciting if this remains a secret as long as possible." She paused for dramatic effect, but I could tell she was just bursting. "The members of the debutante committee have met and, after long deliberation"—she glanced at her vice chairwoman—"have decided on a theme for this year's Magnolia Ball."

A hush fell over the room. You could have heard a pin drop on the perfectly polished hardwood floor.

"That theme," she said, her eyes glittering, "will be Margaret Mitchell's classic novel, and personally one of my favorite movies, *Gone with the Wind*."

A collective squeal rose from the tables, and the room went into a frenzy (or as much of a frenzy as twenty debutantes are capable of whipping up). Some of the girls were clapping. I could have sworn I saw Courtney wipe a tear from her eye. To their credit, Mary Price and Mary Katherine remained fairly calm, although they nodded at each other in mute approval. Taylor clapped her hands together in girly glee.

"Omagosh, y'all," she cried, "that is so perfect!"

"Taylor," Mary Katherine gushed sarcastically, "you can die happy now!"

It seemed I was the only one who had actually lost her appetite. The mini, crustless cucumber sandwiches I had previously been scarfing down no longer looked appealing. Brown had better be worth it, was all I could think.

Finally the announcements came to an end, which was fortunate, since I'd had about as much debutante as I could handle for one day, or for one lifetime, if anyone was asking. As we spilled out of the room, surrounded by girls buzzing with ideas on how the Club could be transformed into Tara, Mary Price turned to me. "So, what are you up to tonight?"

Despite our hockey gossip sessions and Slurpee bonding, I was aware that this was the first time Mary Price had asked me this question. It was a question asked by friends, not hockey friends but *friend*-friends.

My answer was honest but still cautiously sarcastic: "Not much. Rearranging my sock drawer, doing some Facebook stalking, helping my mom change the lint filter on the dryer—the usual."

"Wow, that's a lot of excitement for one night," Mary Price joked. "Well, we heard there's some junior guy who might have people over. We'll probably just end up driving around—that's how it always ends up—but if you want to come . . ."

"Yeah," Taylor interjected, "you should *to*-tally come out with us!"

I told them I guessed I could always DVR the Saturday night Lifetime movie.

"Cool. We can pick you up," said Mary Price.

"*I* can pick you up," said Taylor, rolling her eyes. "I'm sure I'll be driving. I always drive."

TWELVE

A lady does not curse.

You can front all you want
But you can't catch me.
I'm untouchable, bitch,
I'm the P-I-M-P.

The bass was vibrating through my body as the lyrics from Daddy G's latest hit filled Taylor's tiny Honda.

As Mary Price had predicted, there was nothing going on in Beaufort. The junior's parents had caught wind of his party and canceled their trip. Instead, we were "booze cruising" through Beaufort's quiet, suburban neighborhoods.

Never before had I considered driving around aimlessly as "going out." Earlier in the evening, Bliss had made a comment that struck me as funny, even as it flattered me, calling this "the perfect carful, y'all!" Sandwiched between Bliss and MK, who was bouncing along with Daddy G so vigorously that she was uncomfortably close to spilling beer all over us, I wondered if this was some sort of Southern bonding ritual.

"Mary Katherine, can you please keep the beer down?" Taylor pleaded from the front. "I'm really not in the mood to get pulled over." She glanced nervously in the rearview mirror.

"Sorry, T Diddy, you can take tha gangsta outta the 'hood, but not the 'hood outta tha gangsta," Mary Katherine said in what I hoped she knew was a very bad imitation of ghetto speak. She grasped the beer between her knees as she lit a cigarette.

"And don't ash on my car! I can't believe I'm letting you smoke in it anyway."

I had the feeling this wasn't the first time Mary Katherine had coaxed Taylor into having her way.

"Yeah," Mary Price came to Taylor's aid. "You've gotta quit, MK. You're smoking like, a pack a day."

"I am not. Jeez! If I remember correctly, *someone* in this car used to smoke too. Not gonna name any names, but it starts with 'Mary' and ends with 'Price,'" she said, flicking ash out the window. The cigarette butt glowed red in the darkness of the car.

"Yeah, when I was a freshman, because I thought it looked cool."

"Hey, I don't need any help looking cool," said Mary Katherine, gyrating through the R-rated chorus.

Now, I may have been laughing along like this was the

most normal scene in the world, but I was shell-shocked. This was *not* the scenario I'd imagined when picturing a night out with the debs. Yes, I'd seen them drinking and smoking before. Yes, I'd heard Mary Katherine cuss repeatedly. But rapping? *Booze cruising?* Our driver wasn't drinking (Taylor didn't drink; her father said it was sinful), but we certainly were. What if we got pulled over?

"I can't believe you guys listen to rap." The comment escaped my mouth before I realized I was thinking out loud.

"Why?" Mary Price laughed.

"I don't know. I guess I figured you were more the CMT than the BET types."

"Well, we like a little Tupac with our Rascal Flatts. Except for Taylor. She likes Christian rock." Mary Price rolled her eyes. "Beer me, Bliss."

Bliss fished a can out of the dwindling twelve-pack she'd stolen from her parents and passed it over the front seat. "Here, babe."

"So what did your friends in Connecticut listen to?" wondered Mary Price.

"Widespread, Phish, String Cheese, some Dave Matthews."

"String cheese?" Bliss repeated. "That's seriously the name of a band?"

"Were you a dirty hippie?" Mary Katherine winked,

putting her thumb and forefinger to her lips like she was puffing on a joint.

"Did you go to any shows?" Mary Price asked before I could ask MK what her definition of a "dirty hippie" entailed.

"My parents were pretty anal about it. Which, come to think of it, is pretty hypocritical, seeing as they were both probably rolling around in the mud at Woodstock. But I did see Dave at Madison Square Garden a couple times."

"Like Madison Square Garden in New York?" asked an astonished Bliss.

"Yep, that one."

"My parents took me to New York once for Christmas." Taylor almost had to shout to be heard over the music. "We saw the Rockettes. Is that at Madison Square Garden?"

"No, that's Rockefeller Center."

"Oh, well it was really cool. They had live animals on stage in the Nativity scene, like camels and stuff."

Daddy G moaned his last "P-I-M-P" over the stereo, and Mary Price grabbed the iPod, grinning back at me.

"I bet this is more what you expected."

The first few notes of a song I recognized filled the car: "Sweet Home Alabama."

"Woohoo!" hollered Bliss.

"Skynyrd!" Mary Katherine yelled as she tossed her

empty beer can out the window and into a ditch.

I was about to object to the littering, but Taylor had already cranked up the volume till the speakers rattled, and by the end of the first chorus, I found myself singing along at the top of my lungs.

As the final strains of the song faded out, our voices cracking from the effort of singing, Mary Katherine leaned forward and turned down the music.

"All right, girls, I've got an announcement to make." She bowed her head, held up a fresh can, and continued slowly and solemnly. "I have done the impossible. I have succeeded in convincing my mother to let me go on the pill."

"Wait," exclaimed Mary Price. "What?!"

"Yep. Told her my cramps were out of control and my doctor agreed, so she let me get 'em."

"Your cramps aren't that bad," Mary Price said with some skepticism.

Mary Katherine smiled mischievously. "I know."

I'd come to realize there wasn't much MK held sacred. There were very few subjects she wouldn't exploit in the name of shock value. Maybe she loved the attention, or maybe she just liked watching people's eyes widen.

"So does that mean you're gonna—you know?—*do* it with Ryker?" Taylor asked, the disapproval in her voice barely concealed.

"Why do you say it like that?" Mary Katherine shot.

Taylor shrugged. "You know, I just think girls our age shouldn't be on birth control."

"Bliss has been on it since she was like, eight! Thank God," Mary Katherine said, giggling.

"Eff you! Leave me out of this one!" Bliss playfully elbowed Mary Katherine in the ribs.

"Eff you," she teased back. "You can do it, but you can't say it?"

"Mary Katherine!" Taylor screeched. She slammed on the brakes, jerking us all forward.

Whoa, I thought. This was *not* how debs talked. Debs were Southern belles who dropped pleases and thank-you's, not F-bombs. My eyes must have been as wide as Taylor's were narrow, because Mary Katherine immediately backed down.

"Sorry. Crossed the line?"

"Yeah, you could say that," Taylor said curtly, but she started driving again.

"Sorry. But seriously," Mary Katherine continued, "I respect your decision to wait, Taylor. You should respect mine. Ryker and I have been dating for three years." She leaned back in her seat for one pensive moment, then turned to me. "Annie, you're from the liberal North. Are you on bc?"

"Annie, you don't have to answer that," cried Mary Price. "Jeez, Mary Katherine." She let out an uncomfortable laugh. "It's called discretion. Not everyone likes to air their reproductive choices in public."

I was relieved. I was all for frankness, but whether or not I was sexually active was not, I hoped, the business of the debutante court.

"Sorry. *Again*." Mary Katherine threw her hands up in surrender. "But speaking of," she said, an impish smile crossing her face. "Annie, what ever happened with you and Robert?" She waggled her eyebrows up and down suggestively. "I totally caught y'all flirting at school the other day! Did y'all hook up?"

"Yeah, I heard Smalley teasing him about you in chemistry," Bliss added gleefully.

"Great. *Teasing* him for talking to me?" I would have liked to think we were past the playground.

"No! In a good way, like he likes you," Bliss said, clutching my arm in earnest reassurance.

"Well, to answer your question—*no*, we have not hooked up," I said emphatically. After freaking out on him, the last thing I needed was for Robert to think I was spreading rumors that we were somehow an item. "We have not hooked up, and after Bliss's party, I doubt we ever will. I think we are firmly on the friend track."

"What happened?" Mary Katherine was all ears, her gossip glands salivating.

Everyone else was sharing; I guessed my number was up. The girls had invited me into their car—into their world, really—and it was time, I supposed, to let them into mine. I took a deep breath. "God, it was so embarrassing!" I exhaled.

Immediately I hesitated. Did Taylor get offended when people said "God" around her, taking the Lord's name in vain and all? Note to self: Gosh.

But I had already started, and there was no turning back. "Remember how Robert brought me to your party a few weeks ago, Bliss? Well, first of all, I didn't know if it was like, a date or what? And I'd been drinking . . . When he dropped me off, he tried to kiss me, and I freaked out and went off into like, a five-minute monologue about Jake. He probably thought I was a psycho."

"Jake the Snake?" asked Mary Price. That's what the girls had faithfully called him since I'd told them about him and Jamie. "Wow, that *is* embarrassing," she teased.

"Thanks for the show of support."

"Kidding. I've totally done much worse." She waved her hand dismissively and turned back around. "He was probably drunk too."

"I don't think so. Anyway . . ." I trailed off. I had said too much. I could never be a spy. Two beers and I'd trade national security secrets like makeup tips. "It was awkward at first, but now it's back to normal, I guess . . . if that's what you'd call it. . . . I mean, we talk at school, but we've never really like, *hung* out again . . . one-on-one, ya know?" I was tripping over my words, a sure sign of guilt. But what was I guilty of? Liking him?

"Don't worry," assured Mary Price. "He's a cool guy. And he's been broken in. He's used to crazy girls."

"How do you mean?" I asked.

"Mary Price and Robert hooked up sophomore year," Bliss threw out nonchalantly as she searched through her tent-size Louis Vuitton purse. "Where did I put my lip gloss?"

Grrreeeaaat, I thought. Like things weren't already complicated enough.

"Y'all were on and off for like, four months, right?" Bliss continued. "Until you picked Dalton?"

For some reason, my earlier warm-fuzzies for Bliss after her "perfect carful" comment were rapidly cooling.

"We were not 'on and off.' We were never *on*! Robert knew I liked Dalton," Mary Price said defensively. "I just could never look at him that way. It kind of creeped me out. I mean, it's *Robert*. . . . But he's a really nice guy," she added quickly, evidently for my benefit, as she turned to look at me when she said it. "I love Robert. And you should *to*-tally go for it."

I nodded and lowered my window for some fresh air. I felt disappointed for some reason. Disappointed in myself? In Robert? In Mary Price? I didn't know. Just disappointed.

Taylor needed gas and Mary Katherine wanted a Red Bull, so we pulled into a Golden Gallon, where they could both fill up. Taylor left the keys in the ignition, so the car was emitting an irritating, high-pitched beep. Leaning up next to Mary Price, Bliss pulled out the key. "Have y'all thought about your deb party yet?" she asked her.

Apparently, a big ball wasn't celebration enough. Every debutante was also expected to throw a party of her own. It was "suggested" in our reading materials.

"Not yet. I need to get on that," said Mary Price before she was interrupted by her ring-tone rendition of Pachelbel's Canon. "Hang on a sec . . . Hello?"

Bliss fell back into her seat. "You're debbing too, aren't you?" she asked, popping a piece of whitening gum into her mouth.

"Yeah. Not by choice."

Bliss got the confused look she wore a lot, like she was trying to solve a really hard math problem no one else could see. "Why not?"

"It's just not really my thing. It wasn't big where I grew up, but my grandmother really wants me to do it."

"Oh." Bliss was quiet.

"Why aren't you doing it?"

"Well, I would, but I can't. There's some stupid rule that your dad has to be a member of the Heritage Society, which is so dumb because membership is hereditary and the society's like, ancient, so if your family is 'new,' which means they've moved here since like, the Civil War, then you don't stand a chance." She smacked her gum and looked personally insulted.

"That is dumb."

The irritation I felt earlier had dissipated. Bliss wasn't the kind of girl you could stay annoyed with. In fact, I'd taken a real liking to her. Maybe it was due to the fact that she wouldn't be winning any Nobel Prizes, but I felt Bliss was incapable of being insincere. She was an open book, what you saw was what you got. It was refreshing, especially given my recent record with backstabbing liars.

"Yeah, I know! And I can't come to the ball either. That's the worst. If I can't make my debut, I'd at least like to be able to watch my best friends make theirs."

"Why can't you?"

"Because other girls would distract attention from the debutantes." She rolled her eyes. "Anyway, I guess I should see it as a compliment—I mean that I'm a distraction." She smiled weakly, but I could tell it was a sore subject.

As much as I hated to admit it, I could sort of understand what Bliss was feeling. What if all my friends got to do something, and I couldn't just because my family wasn't a member of some stupid old club?

Mary Katherine and Taylor returned to the car, Mary Katherine with a sugar-free Red Bull and a bag of chips in her hand.

"Hey. That was Smalley," said Mary Price, flipping her phone shut. "They're at First Meth."

"Well, let's go," Bliss chirped, reapplying her lip-plumping gloss in the window's reflection. She pressed her lips together and admired her new bee-stung pout.

"First *Meth*?" I asked, truly sure that they did not mean crystal.

"Methodist," explained Mary Price. "Church parking lot. We go there when nothing else is going on."

"You go to a *church* parking lot to drink?" I repeated, making sure I understood.

"It's dark and empty." She shrugged.

"Great," Taylor griped. "Maybe if I'm lucky we'll run into my pastor." But she knew she was outnumbered. "Why do I always end up driving, anyway?" she asked, defeated, as she pulled into the intersection.

Mary Katherine leaned forward and patted her on the shoulder. "Because you're the good one."

A few days later, I was gingerly balancing a full bag of groceries on my hip as I followed my mother up the path to our house. A frost the night before had covered the slate with a crust of delicately veined ice, and it was slippery as I tiptoed to our front door. Sliding my free hand into the freezing metal mailbox, I pulled out the rubber-banded bundle.

I'd been checking the mail religiously for weeks. December may have meant Christmas to everyone else (or debutante launch to others), but to me it meant acceptance or rejection. Every day after school and on

Saturdays, I slid my hand into the mailbox, pulled out a handful of junk mail, bills, and flyers, and rifled through the pile to find that my letter from Brown still had not arrived. Maybe they couldn't find Beaufort, I'd thought ruefully.

But today, like a sign from heaven, on the top of the bundle was an envelope with the world's most perfect return address:

Admission Office
Brown University
45 Prospect Street
Providence, RI 02912

I gasped and dropped the groceries in the front hall. It was a fat envelope, and fat was good. Fat was *very* good.

"It's from Brown!" I yelled louder than I needed to, as my mother was standing right behind me. For a second I panicked, remembering the last time I'd received a letter in the mail—two, actually. Didn't disasters come in threes? Like deaths and plagues? And envelopes addressed to Ann Gordon MacRae? My hands were shaking.

"Well, open it!" my mother cried.

Tearing the envelope open, I unfolded the crisp pages. With the feeling I was teetering on the rim of a large canyon, I held my breath and read:

Dear Miss MacRae,

It is our pleasure to inform you that you have been accepted to join Brown University's Class . . .

The rest was a blur. "I'm going to Brown!" I screamed. My mother threw her arms around me as we both began to uncharacteristically jump up and down in the middle of our living room.

"Let's call your father!" she cried, pulling away.

I nodded, tears streaming down my face. The moment was more bittersweet than I had expected. I was getting out of Beaufort, but at what cost?

THIRTEEN

A lady reserves displays of romantic affection for private moments.

As usual, the church was dark and the parking lot was empty, with the exception of Robert's and Smalley's cars, which were pulled into a dark corner to avoid the lot's floodlights. It was New Year's Eve, and this setting had already started to feel strangely familiar—the backseat of Taylor's car, beer in hand and debs at my side, with the only place to go an abandoned church parking lot.

As we pulled up, the boys waved. They were leaning against Smalley's tailgate and sitting in decrepit lawn chairs he kept in the truck bed for just such occasions. Besides Robert, Smalley, and Ryker, there were two football players, Billy and Chris, and a very tall redhead from my Spanish class named Pearson. By now I recognized all of them and, thanks to Mary Katherine—the encyclopedia of BCD gossip—could even have told you their hookup histories and relative desirability in the Beaufort pecking order.

The sound of classic rock spilled from the truck's cab. It was 11:45, only fifteen minutes until countdown, and the boys were passing a honey-colored bottle of cheap liquor. Judging from the fact it was half empty and Billy had his fleece tied around his head, I figured it had been around the circle a few times already.

"Hey there," Robert said, steadying me and Mary Price as we clambered up onto the truckbed. The feeling of his hand on mine lingered a few moments after he let go.

Ever a gentleman, Smalley handed us two beers from the cooler he was using as a footstool.

"Miss MacRae, Happy New Year," Robert said, cheersing me as I perched on the side of the truck.

I smiled. "Happy New Year."

"So, we've changed your mind?" he asked.

I looked at him curiously.

"You said '*Happy* New Year,'" he explained with a sly smirk. "That means you're anticipating a good one. Could us country bumpkins have turned you from your Yankee pride and made you actually *like* Alabama?"

"Who said I didn't like it?"

He laughed. "You didn't have to."

Maybe my contempt for all things Southern hadn't been as well concealed as I'd originally thought.

"So, have we changed your mind?" he asked again.

"It's not . . . what I expected," I said deliberately.

"In what way?"

"In any way, I guess." I looked Robert directly in the eyes. He held my gaze before nodding, satisfied with my answer.

"Does that mean you'll be sticking around?"

"Past high school?"

He nodded again.

"No." I shook my head definitively. "I got into Brown."

"Congrats," he said with a sudden, unsettling iciness I'd never heard from him before. Sipping his beer, he surveyed the scene on the ground.

"Have you decided yet? About Chapel Hill?" I figured it was the question to ask, the one he was waiting for.

"They decided for me. I didn't get in."

Meekly, I apologized, not knowing the polite protocol for rejection news. (Where was Gram when I actually needed her?)

"Yeah. I blew the math part on my SAT. Go figure. I thought guys were supposed to be better at math. Anyway . . ." he said evasively, "I'm going to widen my net. We'll see."

"Ten!" a distant crowd shouted from the radio. Billy cranked the volume to max. The countdown had begun.

"Nine!" our small band of revelers joined in.

Taylor looked about ready to have a heart attack. "Shhh! Be quiet," she pleaded with Bliss, whose arm was entwined in Mary Katherine's and who was counting at the top of her lungs.

"Eight!"

Mary Katherine grabbed Taylor's arm, pulling her to her other side. Taylor rolled her eyes.

"Seven!"

Mary Price reached down, tugging me and Robert to our feet.

"Six!"

She pulled Pearson up to stand beside her, reaching on her tiptoes to drape her arm over his shoulder. Realizing he would be Mary Price Harding's New Year's kiss, Pearson grinned stupidly.

"Five! . . . Four! . . . Three!" Our counting was reaching a drunken crescendo. I was waiting for a priest to come flying out the church doors to chase us out of the parking lot with a crucifix and holy water when I suddenly realized it was almost midnight on New Year's Eve, and I was standing next to Robert Lee.

"Two!"

I took a deep breath and glanced up at him. He looked back. We both smiled.

"One!" we all shouted in unison. "Happy New Year!"

Smalley tried to plant a boozy kiss on an uncooperative Bliss. Mary Price pecked Pearson on the mouth, probably not the lip-lock he'd been hoping for, while Ryker and Mary Katherine looked like they might not be coming up for air any time soon. And Robert and I . . . looked at each other.

For a second, nothing happened. Then we both went in for the hug, awkwardly going one way and then the other until we figured it out, patting each other on the back in an embrace about as passionate as one I'd reserve for my cousin. Releasing, we quickly looked away from each other and were saved when Billy chose the moment to light a sparkler for a lap around the cars, the fleece still tied around his head flapping comically behind him.

Bliss and Taylor, who had given up on keeping everyone quiet, swayed back and forth as they began to sing "Auld Lang Syne" with the radio.

"Should old acquaintance be forgot, and never brought to mind . . ." we all joined.

Though I'd heard the song at least eighteen times before, I'd never really listened to the words. But there, on that warm New Year's Eve in Beaufort, Alabama, they made me think. Which was worse: living in the past, or living in the South? For almost five months I had pitched the two against each other, with the constant fear that forgetting "old acquaintances" meant forgetting myself. Maybe, I thought, looking around the group, this new year was time for resolution.

FOURTEEN

A lady knows which fork to use.

"You can do it," Mary Price coaxed. "You can do it. . . ."

The steaming, golden nugget was just inches from my mouth, but I couldn't bring it closer. Maybe it was the name that turned me off: okra—a word that sounded about as appetizing as brussels sprouts.

Mary Price, Robert, Smalley, and I were among the last holdouts in the lunchroom, waiting for the fourth-period bell to ring. Somehow, the topic had arisen that I had never eaten okra. For kids who had apparently grown up with this staple regularly rotated through their cafeteria menu, this was an unthinkable revelation. Smalley had immediately dared me to eat one. I had counter-dared that I would—if he ate the cottage cheese Jell-O salad. I had sorely underestimated him, as Smalley had wolfed down the electric-green dessert in under two seconds. Now it was my turn.

It didn't help that Robert was sitting next to me,

intently staring at the fried hunk of vegetable as it made its way from my plate to my mouth and hovered there.

I glanced sideways at him. "You're sure there are no freak okra allergies?"

"Quit stalling," he directed. "A dare's a dare."

I looked nervously to Mary Price on my other side. "I hope you're prepared for me to throw up."

"I'll be here to hold your hair."

I took a deep breath as Smalley started clapping and chanting, "Do it, do it, do it!"

Closing my eyes, I pinched my nose, opened my mouth, and slid the greasy morsel off my fork with my teeth. It landed on my tongue with a slight burned taste. I bit down. The okra oozed, the approximate consistency of fried boogers. Swallowing it almost whole, I chased it with a full glass of Mr. Pibb.

My three companions cheered as I stuck my tongue out, *Survivor*-style, to show that the okra had gone down the hatch. Smalley gave me a high-five from across the table, and Mary Price rubbed my back as I coughed and spluttered.

"That's my girl," Robert said, hugging his arm around my neck.

Smiling from ear to ear, I tried not to gag.

"There is nothing more attractive or appreciated in a woman than good manners."

Once again, I found myself at the mercy of the Heritage Society's Debutante Planning Committee. On this crisp January day, the debs were sitting, cross-legged and straight-backed, on well-appointed but slightly worn wing chairs and antique divans in one of the society's fine salons. Seated on a velvet couch between Taylor and Mary Price, I took in our torturess du jour. She was a conservative but attractively dressed young brunette appropriately named Susan Grammer, an etiquette expert brought in specially for our benefit all the way from Atlanta.

"Unfortunately, etiquette is a lost art," Ms. Grammer continued. With legs crossed at her thin ankles and hands clasped primly in her lap, she looked around the circle of debutantes. To her left was a small table covered with a white tablecloth and elaborately set with more silver than Tiffany's showroom. "In today's world, people rarely take the time to extend common courtesy to their friends, their family, their acquaintances, to say the least, strangers. With so much to do, we dash off to our meetings or to our yoga classes and tell ourselves we'll write that thank-you note later."

We do?

"Rather than take the extra effort to get out the good china for our dinner guests," she went on, "we make do with our everyday tableware."

I don't *have* good china, I mentally protested. I'm eight-freakin-teen.

"It's a shame," lamented Ms. Grammer, a single strand of hair falling across her creased brow, "because it tells people that we don't care. It shows a lack of respect for them and ultimately for ourselves. Some may say that etiquette is old-fashioned or trivial, but when etiquette goes out the window, civility soon follows." She self-consciously brushed the stray hair back into her bun.

All around the room, blond heads were bobbing in inspired agreement. At least maybe I'd finally figure out what to do with all those demitasse spoons, I thought, craning my neck to count the sixteen pieces of crystal, china, and silver that made up the place setting to shame all place settings.

"But etiquette is not just about the details," Ms. Grammer intoned. "The legendary Emily Post once said, 'Nothing is less important than which fork you use. Etiquette is the science of living.'"

Twenty minutes later, we were learning which fork to use. For the record, the salad fork lies farthest from the plate only when the salad is served first, American style, and while dessert *spoons* may be placed at the top of the charger plate, at formal dinners, dessert *forks* are usually served with the dessert plate. Don't even get me started on finger bowls. To make matters that much more excruciating, Courtney kept raising her hand to ask questions, like she was worried she might actually one day be in charge of seating arrangements at a White House dinner. Within the hour, I also knew how to properly word a handwritten response cordially declining or accepting a wedding invitation and how to sit so as not to show my undergarments. I also knew the proper way to go to the bathroom.

"Please excuse me while I go to the ladies' room," I whispered, just as we'd been taught, to Mary Price.

"Please, dear, wait and I'll join you," whispered Mary Price in mock seriousness.

We tiptoed out, edging along the back of the room to the door, careful to avoid the eagle-eyed gaze of Totty Patterson.

"If I tell you something, can you keep a secret?" I asked when we were safely in the bathroom. Plunking myself down into one of the cushy powder-room chairs, I kicked off my clogs.

"Sure," answered Mary Price as she leaned against the faux marble counter. In the rosy glow of the vanity lights, she looked wholesome and luminous, like a girl in a soap commercial.

"I hate this stuff."

Mary Price smiled understandingly. "If I tell *you* a secret, can you keep it?"

"Sure."

"I'm the queen."

"I'm guessing you don't mean drag queen."

"That'd be awesome," Mary Price said with a chuckle.

"I'd love to see Mrs. Patterson's face if I showed up at the Magnolia Ball in full drag. But no, there's a queen of the debutante court."

"What does that mean?"

"I look pretty and smile and lead the ball."

"Congratulations?" I offered facetiously.

"Yeah." Mary Price rolled her eyes. "It's supposed to be an honor."

"So what's the problem? You don't want to be queenie?"

Mary Price stared down at her high-heeled boots. "I just kind of feel like I cheated, like I didn't earn it."

"Why?" I asked, confused. How did anyone *earn* it?

"My mom was queen. And my dad is 'historian' or something at the Heritage Society."

"So?"

"I don't know. I guess I think it should go to someone who really cares, ya know?"

"Like Taylor?" I asked, raising an eyebrow.

"Yeah, I guess. Like Taylor."

"So you don't care?"

She paused and looked torn, like she might be trying to decide on the spot. "I don't know," she said finally. "I do, I think . . . but sometimes I don't. Does that make sense?"

"No," I said with a straight face. "I'm kidding. Yes, it does, totally."

In some ways, Mary Price's feelings sounded a lot like my own toward Beaufort. I didn't like it . . . but maybe I did. . . . Although I certainly didn't like that I maybe liked it. Just thinking about it gave me a headache.

Suddenly the bathroom door swung open and Mary Katherine appeared.

"What are y'all doing in here?" she asked suspiciously.

"Powdering our noses," Mary Price answered. She turned to inspect her hair and makeup.

MK looked between us in the mirror, like someone who had just walked in on two people talking about her. "Well, it's almost handshake time," she warned as she pushed open a bathroom stall.

"Yeah, we should go," Mary Price said.

I followed her out, with one burning question on my mind: *What the hell was "handshake time"?*

FIFTEEN

A lady does not telephone a gentleman.

If there is one day masterminded to give teenage girls premature ulcers, it is Valentine's Day. I couldn't stand the day that lets greeting-card companies exploit the already self-conscious and boy-obsessed. And if that weren't bad enough, in our artificially depressed state, we are surrounded by profane amounts of chocolate—as if consuming my own weight in saturated fats is going to boost my chances of getting a Valentine the next go-round. I had *never* been a fan, but now, single once again, I truly loathed it.

Country Day, however, was not going to let me forget it. The school had a unique twist on the standard "send your Valentine an anonymous carnation" fundraiser. Rather than the puny pink and white filler flowers, students could send their crushes a can of Crush soda, an addictively sweet, orange-flavored drink I had just recently discovered through Mary Katherine. All day girls stood in front of the message board, abandoned ships on the sea of love searching in vain for the note that told them they were pretty, they were worthy, they were loved, and to prove it, they could come to the switchboard to pick up their can of orange soda. Those girls lucky enough to receive these unlikely tokens of affection nursed their lukewarm beverages throughout the day, displaying them like badges of honor.

Never had a soft drink caused so much heartache, I thought as I glanced at the board on my way to lunch. Pathetic.

Then I spotted it. Or, I thought I did: my name on a slip of paper pinned at the bottom of the M–Q column. I did a reluctant double take, nonchalantly bending down to peer at the note: "Ann Gordon MacRae."

I felt the color in my cheeks rise as I glanced around, waiting for someone to start laughing at their hilariously unfunny practical joke. Finding only a furtive, jealous glance from a short blonde inspecting the R–T's, I took down the note and opened it: "Happy Valentine's Day. Someone has a Crush on you!"

Refolding the paper and stuffing it into my cords pocket, I tried to walk casually to the switchboard, but my heart was pounding. Was it from who I hoped it was from? Did I actually hope it was from him? Or had my dad caught wind of the Crush sale? That would be both totally embarrassing and totally predictable.

I smiled at the moley receptionist who had greeted me my first day, then joined four other girls searching for their names scrawled in cursive on the pink paper hearts paper-clipped to the can tabs. Finding mine, I extracted the note from the can and unconsciously held my breath as I read the message handwritten inside:

For a lady on Valentine's Day

That was it. No signature, no clues, just that: "For a lady on Valentine's Day." My mind instantly raced through possibilities. It didn't sound like my dad. Jake would never . . . Could it be . . . No, I shouldn't jump to conclusions, I thought, wiping the hope from my head. I needed a second opinion, and a third and a fourth. I headed for the dining hall.

"Omagosh, that's definitely a guy's handwriting," Taylor concluded, returning the slip of paper to me. Bliss and Mary Price had already examined the evidence and concurred. Mary Katherine's opinion I'd have to get later, as she was in the library cramming for a test.

"Well, short of asking every guy at Country Day to submit a handwriting sample, I don't think that does me much good," I sighed, popping the top of my Crush can.

Mary Price pushed her plate of tater tots and gray,

gelatinous turkey across the table. "Seriously, y'all, this is gross," she announced, then looking up, added, "I bet it's from Robert."

My stomach fluttered.

"Omagosh, it's totally Robert!" Bliss confirmed, spreading her manicured hands on the table and conspiratorially leaning in.

Mary Price nodded. "But what's the 'lady' stuff about?"

I thought back to our conversation in Robert's car, the night of Bliss's party. It felt like ages ago. Could he really remember that?

"I think it's romantic," said Bliss. "*I* haven't gotten a Crush this year," she added with a pout, crossing her arms over her ample chest.

"Well, that just evens it out for the three you've gotten every other year," said Mary Price, crunching the ice from her drink between her teeth.

"Yeah, but they were all from dorks!"

"I just wish I knew who it was," I said, not ready to change the conversation from speculation on my Crush to Bliss's recent dry spell. "It would help, seeing as I *still* haven't found a second escort."

My dad had insisted I ask Virginia and Charlotte's brother, Richard, to be an escort, which I for once had no objections to, as there were no other candidates applying for the job. Unfortunately, he was my only male cousin, and the second slot was yet to be filled.

"Maybe I could ask Crush Guy." I glanced at Taylor and Mary Price to gauge their reaction to the idea.

"You still haven't turned in the names of your escorts?" Taylor asked with alarm. "They were due last week!"

"I know. I know," I groaned. "I keep hoping if I put it off, it'll go away. Maybe I should just order a professional escort out of the Yellow Pages and be done with it."

"That would be perfect." Mary Price grinned. "I'll chip in."

"Deal."

"All right," Mary Price said, pushing back her chair and picking up her tray. "I gotta run. I have to finish my biology lab before class. I'll see y'all later."

"Bye," Bliss and Taylor chimed after her.

"Later," I said.

"Annie, why don't you just invite Robert to be your escort? Crush or no Crush," Taylor asked.

To be honest, I'd been wondering the same thing. But the memories of my freak-out in the car and our exquisitely awkward moment at New Year's still haunted me. I had said I just wanted to be friends. What if that was all he wanted now? Would asking him to be my escort just be begging for punishment?

"I thought about it. I just don't know. Would he think that's weird? I mean, I've only known him for six months. Isn't it supposed to be someone you like, took baths with as a kid?"

"Well, you've got your cousin, right?" Taylor asked.

"Yeah."

"Then you can totally ask a friend. You're just not supposed to ask boyfriends."

"Yeah, why is that?" I had wondered about that tidbit of information I'd read in our deb bible.

"In case you break up," Taylor explained. "One year there was a huge scene 'cause a deb asked her boyfriend to be her escort, and they got into this massive fight at the ball. She caught him in the bathroom with her little sister. Everyone was talking about it."

"Well, as I have no boyfriend, I have no problem with that rule."

"You've got a secret admirer now. That's way better than a boyfriend, if you ask me," said Bliss. "Much more romantic."

While I could have continued our Crush conversation for several hours—after all, it had been a while—the lunchroom was clearing out for fourth period. Dumping our trays on the conveyor belt, we headed toward the cafeteria's glass doors. My heart jumped when I saw who was coming through them.

"Hi, Robert," said Taylor in a singsong voice.

"Taylor. Bliss," Robert acknowledged as they slipped past him. Behind his back, they smiled at me.

"Hey," I managed, my stomach twisting in nervous knots.

"Hey, lady." He winked. "Gotta grab something to eat before class." Sliding past me, he casually put his hand on my arm.

"*Lady?!*" mouthed Bliss and Taylor simultaneously. I felt my face take on a nice beet color.

"*Shut up,*" I mouthed back, and pushed them down the hall, a smile spreading across my face.

Okay, I reasoned that evening in my room, technically, I had no choice. Mrs. Patterson had called my house to kindly remind me that the deb committee needed the names of my two escorts for the newspaper and programs. I had to ask someone; why not Robert? We talked in school and out. Despite the occasional—okay, recurrent—awkward moments, you couldn't deny that our interactions tended toward the flirtatious. *And*, he *had* called me "lady" today. He was clueing me in, right? Still, I was hesitant. What was the point of getting wrapped up in someone here? All a boy had gotten me last time was a big, fat, broken heart and an ex-best friend. Sure, Robert was cute, but he wasn't even my type. He liked football. He hunted. He was from *Ala-bama*—bless his heart!

I stared at the school directory that had been lying open on my desk at "Lee, Robert" for half an hour. I didn't have his cell number, so if I did this, it had to be old-school. I started to dial the number and hung up. All right, Annie, I thought. Game face. Before I could psyche myself out, I punched the numbers again. Dancing around my room in circles, I bit my nails, switching fingers with each ring. Please go to voice mail, please go to voice mail, I chanted. No wait! Then I would have to leave a message. That could be bad. Too much room for error. I could hang up. *But what if they had caller ID?*

"Lee residence," a woman's voice answered.

I froze. "Hi, may I please speak with Robert?" I asked in my newfound parent voice. My heart pounded.

"Just a minute," she said pleasantly. I could hear the phone click on a hard surface as she set it down and went to find him.

I was biting my lip now, and though it had been months since I'd dropped Jamie's ring in an envelope and mailed it back without a note, I was still nervously rubbing the spot where it had once been. Realizing what I was doing, I stopped and sat on my hand. A moment later, a familiar voice came over the line.

"Hello?"

"Hey, Robert. It's Annie . . . MacRae."

"Annie who?"

My stomach dropped to the floor. *Abort! Abort!* a voice in my head screamed. There was a stunned silence like a canyon between us.

"Um, Annie MacRae," I stammered, "from school. Uh, we're in English together?"

Robert started laughing. "I'm kidding, Annie MacRae. I know who you are."

"You jerk!" The sailor's knot that my stomach had worked itself into loosened a tiny fraction.

"What's up?"

"Not much," I answered, lying back on my bed. "What are you up to?"

"Watching the basketball game."

"Do you want me to call you back?" I asked hesitantly, really hoping I wouldn't have to find the guts to do this again.

"No, that's okay. I'm DVR-ing it."

"Oh, cool. Wish we had that." *Here goes.* It was like jumping into a cold pool, I thought. If I just closed my eyes, by the time I felt it, it'd be over. "Actually, I was calling to ask you something. I was wondering if you'd like to be one of my escorts for the deb ball?" I held my breath, anticipating a silence as he tried to come up with a polite excuse.

"I'd love to," he answered immediately.

"Really?"

"Hell yeah! I wouldn't miss seeing Ann Gordon MacRae curtsy in a big, white dress to save my life."

There was something definitely adorable in the way he said it: "mah life."

"Are you teasing me?" I asked playfully. "'Cause if so, then the offer's off the table."

"I would never tease you! As your escort, it's actually my duty to defend your honor."

Some time later I hung up the phone. I looked at the clock. Robert and I had talked for over an hour and a half; I couldn't even remember what about—school, Connecticut, Brown, *Entourage*, even his dad—but it was nice, natural, easy.

I had to tell someone. Once upon a time, it would have been Jamie. Not anymore. But there *was* someone who would understand—Mary Price was the closest thing I had to a confidante these days. It was too late to call, so I texted her instead: ASKD ROBRT 2 B MY ESCORT.

Two minutes later my phone beeped with a new message: ATTA GRL!!!

SIXTEEN

*A lady always dresses
for the occasion.*

"Lady Slipper?" I read the cursive writing on the store's pink-and-white-striped awning as Mary Price pulled into the parking lot that fronted a strip of shops off Azalea Avenue. We were meeting Mary Katherine, Taylor, and our "fashion consultant" Bliss to search for deb dresses.

Three mannequins modeled voluminous wedding gowns in the store window, the middle one sporting a sparkling tiara. "Wait. Is this a bridal shop?" I asked, horrified.

"Yep. They have the most *adorable* dresses," Mary Price said, the door tinkling behind us as we went in. Bliss and Mary Katherine were already inside, picking through racks of white satin, silk, and chiffon.

"Y'all are late," Mary Katherine announced without turning.

"Sorry," Mary Price apologized. "I was starving, so we made a detour—"

Her explanation was cut short as Taylor emerged from the dressing room in a gown whose layers upon layers of tulle made the skirt stand out in a full, four-foot circle, like a great white bouffant. She twirled.

"Whooaa," Mary Katherine exclaimed.

"What?" Taylor asked, peering down at the dress.

"Way too poofy."

"You look like Mother Ginger from the *Nutcracker*." Bliss giggled.

Taylor considered herself in the mirror, then nodded her head in agreement.

"I can't believe I'm eighteen and shopping for a wedding dress. This is so Alabama," I moaned.

"Hey, watch it," joked Mary Price, admiring a halter dress from the Vera Wang section.

Taylor clucked. "Don't tell me you never fantasized about what you want your wedding dress to look like. We get *two* chances!"

"Not that I would ever admit publicly. I do think I want something strapless, though. I heard it makes your boobs look bigger. Hey, what about this one?" I asked, pulling out a hip-skimming silk dress with a mini train that puddled in the back. "Cute, right?"

"Sorry, babe," said Mary Price. "Has to be big and puffy. At the very *least* A-line."

"Y'all have so many rules!" I cried in exasperation, hanging the offending dress back on the rack.

Mary Price looked at me sideways. "'Y'all?'"

"I mean, *youz guyz*." I exaggerated my supposed accent the girls never failed to point out.

"They're not rules . . ." corrected Taylor, disappearing again behind the dressing room's cherry pink curtains.

". . . they're traditions," Mary Price finished for her.

"Spoken like a true queen," MK remarked tartly from one of the store's large, white divans on which she languidly reclined. At the moment she looked more the part herself.

"Shut up," sighed Mary Price.

Ignoring them, I surveyed the store and in the corner, spied a headless mannequin wearing a simple, one-shoulder dress. "I kind of like this one," I said, standing next to it so they could imagine it on.

"Asymmetrical necklines are out," Mary Katherine declared as she thumbed disinterestedly through a bridal magazine. "Besides, the deb committee wouldn't approve it."

"Oh." I wondered if I should be bothered by her curtness. Had my lack of fashion sense so offended Mary Katherine? "The committee has to approve our dresses?"

"We have to send them pictures," Taylor explained, returning from the dressing room in her civilian clothes. "They just wanna make sure no one has sequins or crazy cleavage or something."

"Or a one-shoulder neckline?" I asked.

"Exactly."

"Oooh!" Bliss cooed from the far corner of the room. She turned, holding a gown out in front of her. "Annie, this would look sooo cute on you!"

The dress was strapless, stylish but simple with a high waist accented by a cream sash.

"Oh, that is cute," I agreed. "I'll try it on."

"Isn't that the one you were looking at the other day?" Mary Katherine asked Mary Price over the top of her magazine.

"Yeah, but that's okay. Annie, you try it on." Mary Price waved me toward the dressing rooms.

"You sure?" I asked hesitantly, the dress now in my hands.

"Yeah, of course."

"I think it's too white for your skin tone," said Mary Katherine pointedly. "You need a creamier white. You'll look washed out."

"O-kay," I murmured, totally confused by Mary Katherine's suddenly snarky tone. I'd witnessed her turn on unwitting victims before, but I'd never been a target myself.

"Try it," Mary Price urged. "You never know what it'll look like until you see it on." As I reluctantly headed for the dressing room, I saw her shoot Mary Katherine a puzzled look.

"MK, what's wrong with you?" she whispered as I undressed.

"Nothing," Mary Katherine replied in a voice loud enough for even the stock girl to hear.

"You're being kind of bitchy."

"No, I'm not. I just pointed out that that was the dress you were looking at," Mary Katherine said defensively.

"I don't care if Annie tries it on. There are like, two hundred dresses here, and my mom is thinking I should get mine made anyway."

"Whatever. You'd give Annie your right lung if she asked for it."

"What are you talking about?" Mary Price asked, sounding genuinely bewildered.

"Y'all are inseparable these days. You're like, totally attached at the hip."

"Seriously, what are you talking about?" Mary Price demanded. "I hang out with you as much as I do with her."

Within full earshot of the entire conversation, I was uncomfortable. Should I come out and confront Mary Katherine or huddle in the dressing room and pretend I didn't hear? Zipping up the side of the dress, I turned to see myself in the mirror. The dress was gorgeous, but under the harsh overhead light, dark shadows pooled under my eyes and nose, making me look slightly sinister.

Outside, the two Marys were still arguing in barely hushed tones. "Give me an example of how Annie and I are 'attached at the hip.'" Mary Price's bafflement was quickly turning to anger.

"Whatever. Forget I said anything."

Unable to hide in the dressing room much longer without arousing the suspicion of the saleslady, I stepped out from behind the taffeta curtain. Everyone turned to look, Mary Katherine quickly refocusing her attention on *Modern Bride*. For a few awkward seconds, no one said anything. I could hear the silver clock on the sales desk ticking.

"You look so gorgeous!" Taylor finally exclaimed. *Thank you, Taylor.* "Doesn't she look gorgeous?"

"You do. Annie, you should totally get it," Mary Price insisted.

I glanced at the price tag. "Yeah, well it better be gorgeous. It's three thousand dollars!"

"That's not that much for a Monique Lhuillier," Mary Katherine noted without looking up.

"Well, it's a lot for an Annie MacRae," I snapped back.

"Maybe you could get somebody to make one like it?" Taylor offered.

"Yeah, maybe." But I didn't want the dress anymore. Retreating behind the curtain, I hung up the small silk fortune and yanked on my jeans and T-shirt. So much for a fun day of shopping. How had Mary Katherine gone from friend to frenemy in sixty seconds flat?

"Guys, I'm not really feeling well. I think I'm gonna go home," I said when I stepped back out of the dressing room.

"Yeah, I think I'm gonna head too," said Bliss. Apparently the sour mood in the store had gotten to her as well. "Do you want a ride?"

We hadn't been in the car thirty seconds before Bliss's lip started to quiver and tears sprang to her eyes.

"What's wrong?" I asked, alarmed. I thought I was having the bad day.

"I don't know. Looking at all those dresses . . ." She paused, trying to choke back tears. "It just makes me sad. I mean, I want to deb *so* bad, and it sucks watching all of y'all get to do it when I can't. It's so unfair!"

With that, Bliss erupted into full-on sobs. Her face contorted into such a look of pained desperation, I was afraid she might run us off the road and end it all.

"Don't cry, Bliss," I pleaded. "Seriously, it probably looks fun from the outside, but it's really just a pain in the ass. It's taking up all our time."

"I know!" she wailed. "But I want it to take up *my* time, too."

Okay, what to do? I wasn't good with crying people. Be comforting, I thought.

"Bliss, really, it's not worth getting upset over. It's just some stupid party where girls get to play princess for a day and parents get to show off their money."

Bliss, gripping the steering wheel like it might run away from her, turned to me wild-eyed, her brow screwed up in a look of genuine horror.

"It's not *stupid*, Annie! You don't get it." She was obviously disturbed by my disrespect for the institution. "It's really special. You get to be part of this tradition that's gone on for like, *hundreds* of years. It's one of those moments you'll always remember, like your wedding or when your kids are born. . . ." She started to melt down again. "It's your friends and family and *everyone* all celebrating you and how much they love you and how special you are. You're lucky to be a part of it, and you don't even realize it."

This sent her into another bout of blubbering. Popping the glove compartment, I searched for a tissue or napkin—anything to soak up the rivulets flowing from her eyes and nose.

"I'm sorry, Bliss," I conceded, handing her a crumpled fast-food napkin. "I guess I am lucky, and I should be more aware of that." As I said it, I realized with a pang of guilt that it was probably true.

Bliss's shoulders continued to heave in suppressed sobs as she tried to quiet herself. "It just seems so unfair sometimes. But I shouldn't let that distract from y'all's happiness." She wiped the mascara off her cheeks. "You really should enjoy it while you can, Annie. You'll look back one day and wish you had."

By the time we pulled up to my house, Bliss was blotchy but composed.

"Thank you, Bliss," I said, leaning over the console to give her a hug. "For everything."

"Sure." She smiled meekly. "What are friends for?"

I didn't respond. But inside the answer tickled my brain—friends, evidently, were for reminding you to take your head out of your ass every once in a while.

SEVENTEEN

A lady is mindful of the needs of others.

Every April *The Beaufort Bugle* ran photos of the debutante court. And every year the Debutante Planning Committee specifically requested that the paper include pictures from the debs' visit to the children's hospital, or so I had been told in one of my countless deb meetings.

Knowing Gram would freak if her granddaughter were in the paper wearing something she deemed "inappropriate," I had asked Mary Price to come over and help me pick out an outfit. We'd decided on tan pants (Mary Price had vetoed white before Memorial Day) with a lacy, pink tank (feminine and fun), and a light, fitted blazer (conservative and mature) borrowed from Mary Price's closet. Not exactly me, but the outfit was cute and, I hoped, beyond Gram's recrimination. With weekly calls for transparent reasons (could my father help her change a lightbulb; oh, and had I found proper shoes?), my grandmother had been keeping close tabs on my debutante development.

Safely attired, I found myself, along with the rest of the court, entering the hospital's sliding glass doors. The large, gray building's dull exterior disguised a surprisingly colorful interior decorated with balloons, stickers, and cardboard cartoon cutouts. Our troupe of young ladies was led to a large, clinical version of a playroom, where patients and some nurses were playing board games and watching television. Many of the kids had lost their hair, and some were small and alarmingly fragile. All of them looked like they'd seen better days.

But when they saw us coming, the children's faces brightened. Some of the younger ones ran up to us, grabbing our hands and clinging to our legs.

A smiling nurse wearing a yellow uniform with clowns on it welcomed us. "Hi there! They've been waitin' for y'all."

Earlier that morning I'd been complaining to my mother that the trip was nothing but a blatant publicity stunt, an attempt to justify the outrageous party in July. Now, watching a five-year-old girl clasp on to Taylor's leg, I felt like a horrible person. These kids certainly weren't here for a photo op.

"We're so glad you could have us," Totty Patterson said, shaking the nurse's hand. "I'm Totty and these are our debutantes."

"I'm Nurse Brenda—or that's what the kids call

me. But y'all can just call me Brenda." She chuckled cheerfully. "Come on in."

We moved into the room, joining the kids in their ongoing games of Sorry and Clue. The other girls mixed in seamlessly—all the social graciousness hammered into them over the years paying off, I supposed—but I, the newest to this world, felt momentarily lost. Until I spotted a boy by himself at a plastic-covered card table. He wore a green bathrobe over plaid pajamas and was sitting in a wheelchair. He was bald, I assumed from the chemo, which, judging from the dark circles that ringed his eyes, had been recent.

"Hi," I said, attempting cheeriness as I sat down in the folding chair next to him.

"Hi," he answered. He sounded as if speaking was an effort.

"I'm Annie. What's your name?"

"Henry," he mumbled, looking up at me with glassy, brown eyes.

"Can I help you with your puzzle, Henry?" It was a picture of the Statue of Liberty.

"Sure."

Like a pro, Henry had put the puzzle's border together first and was now working his way in.

I picked up a piece of pedestal. "You know, I used to live near New York."

"Really?" Henry's eyes widened with interest.

"Yeah. My parents took me to see the Statue of Liberty when I was about your age. You're what, like, eight?" I asked as I tried to fit the piece.

"I turned ten last week." He popped his piece easily into place. He was little for ten. "My parents told me when I'm better they're gonna take me to New York. They gave me this puzzle and said for my next birthday we'll see it in real life."

"That's awesome."

The more we talked, the more animated Henry became. He said his mother was a teacher at a school for special kids. His dad was a bus driver. Two years ago they'd found out he had leukemia. This was his second round of chemotherapy, and he'd been at Grace for two months now. He liked it okay. It was nice having other kids around to play with, better than the grown-up hospitals. Plus, they had cool toys. But he missed his dog, Sam, and his Little League team.

Lady Liberty had her crown and a torch by the time Nurse Brenda called everyone for cookies and juice. I pushed Henry's wheelchair into the adjacent dining room, finding a spot for us at a long table covered with a rainbow-colored tablecloth and potted daisies. I left him to get us some cookies from the refreshment table and was not happy to discover Mary Katherine at the punch bowl.

It had been almost three weeks since our run-in at

the dress shop. We weren't exactly *avoiding* each other, mainly because we couldn't—now that we were friends, we were expected to share a lunch table every day—but there was undeniable tension that I chose to handle by staying civil yet aloof. We did what we could to not speak directly to each other. It had worked so far, but the peace wouldn't last. Which was going to make our upcoming deb party problematic, to say the least.

Shortly after New Year's, the Marys and Taylor had asked me to cohost their deb party with them. Apparently time spent booze cruising and bonding over etiquette classes had solidified me in the crew. After months of planning—most of which, except for location (Belmont had of course been offered by Gram), had been eagerly done by Mary Price's and Taylor's moms—the party was now in just two short weeks. Which didn't leave me and Mary Katherine a lot of time to curtsy and make up.

"Hey, MK," I said flatly.

"Hi." Mary Katherine returned my greeting with as much enthusiasm as I had granted her.

"This is pretty intense, huh?" I politely plowed on. "I thought it was just a photo op."

"I came in middle school with my confirmation class," said Mary Katherine. "I remember it was depressing."

I nodded.

"What'd you end up doing about an escort, by

the way?" she asked, nibbling around the edge of a pretzel-shaped cookie. I realized just how much we hadn't talked the past few weeks. I had assumed she knew.

"I thought I told you. I asked Robert."

"Robert? You did?" Mary Katherine acted surprised.

"Yeah. Why do you say it like that?" I replied warily.

"It's not a big deal," she said, dismissing it with a shrug of a shoulder. "I was just wondering if Mary Price was okay with it, that's all."

"Why would Mary Price have a problem with it?"

"Just 'cause they used to hook up and are so close now." She balled the remainder of her cookie in a napkin that she tossed on the table.

"But I thought that was forever ago, and Mary Price just sees him as a friend." I was confused. I thought we had covered this.

"Yeah, that's what she says. . . ." Mary Katherine shrugged again, brushing the cookie crumbs from her hands. "Anyway, I'm *sure* she doesn't care. I just know I would want someone to ask me first."

I was half pissed at Mary Katherine's passive-aggressive bullshit and half nervous that there was some truth to what she was saying. What if it *had* bothered Mary Price that I'd asked Robert? We'd talked about it, but I'd never outright asked her permission. I didn't think I needed it.

"Well, I better get back to my kid," said Mary Katherine,

leaving me at the punch bowl, her mission to put me in my place accomplished.

I tried to think back to any time Mary Price might have seemed less than happy with my choice of escort. As I searched my memory, Nurse Brenda shuffled up.

"Henry's a sweetie, isn't he?" she asked, ladling herself some fruit punch.

"Yeah," I said, snapping out of it. "He's a real trouper."

"He is. He's really fought this. You know, his parents have tried to be very honest with him. He knows it doesn't look good, but he just refuses to give up. We could all learn a thing or two from a child like that."

"It doesn't look good?" I asked, feeling sucker punched. How selfish was I? Henry had real problems and I was worrying about a high school catfight.

"Most kids recover with treatment, but his cancer was pretty advanced. They think they got it all, but that's what they thought last time too," she said with a sigh.

"Oh," I murmured. What was there to say? "Well, I'm gonna take these over." I dumbly held up a plate of sugar-free sugar cookies.

I sat down next to Henry, my head swimming in a sea of emotions. "Here we go," I said, setting the plate of cookies in front of him.

"What is a debutante anyway?" Henry asked, crunching on his cookie and scattering crumbs all over the front of his clean bathrobe.

"Well," I said, smiling at the very pertinent question, "I'm just learning the answer to that question myself, Henry."

"You're just a bunch of girls who go around and visit sick kids?"

"We do a little bit of that. We also take a few classes on having good manners and dancing. Then we have a big party where we raise money for the hospital." The explanation finally rang true to me.

"That sounds fun. Wish I could be a debutante," he said thoughtfully.

I laughed and stifled the urge to offer him my spot. Instead I told him he could be an honorary escort, at which he beamed, pleased with the title.

The *Bugle* photographer was making his rounds through the dining room, his 35-millimeter poised for moments like this one. Seeing our smiles, he approached. "Y'all mind if I take a picture?" he asked, already raising the camera to his eye.

"Sure!" Henry piped.

I lightly draped my arm over Henry's shoulders, which felt thin and bony under his robe, and we smiled for the camera like old friends.

"Is this gonna be in the paper?" Henry asked, a hopeful smile spreading across his pallid face.

"Well, I can't promise that this one will make it, but it may," the photographer replied.

"Cool," Henry said, satisfied with the man's maybe.

Mrs. Patterson stood and clapped her hands. "Okay, girls and boys. I'm sorry to break this up, since we're all having fun," she announced in her prim drawl, "but I'm afraid it's time for the debutantes to make their way upstairs for lunch with members of the hospital board."

As some of the kids let out a disappointed "Awww," we said our good-byes, some of us offering hugs, all of us offering hopes that they would get well soon.

"It was nice meeting you, Henry." It hurt my heart that I had to leave him here in a hospital, instead of outside, playing with his dog or his friends, as he should have been.

"Annie?" he asked tentatively.

"Yeah?"

"Will you send me a copy of our picture in the newspaper—if it makes it?"

A lump suddenly rose in my throat, and I wished very much that the picture would make it, that I could call the photographer or the editor and make sure, somehow, that Henry would see his photo in *The Beaufort Bugle*.

"Sure, Henry."

"I'll put it on the bulletin board in my room."

"That'd be nice," I said, "but you also have to promise me something."

"What?"

"You'll send me a postcard from the Statue of Liberty."

"Okay." He grinned. "Deal."

I barely touched my dinner that night. Dad had gotten takeout from No. 1 China Buffet, but between thinking about Henry and what Mary Katherine had said at the hospital, I'd lost my appetite. Engrossed in a stimulating conversation about some ultraconservative history cabal at Queen Anne's, my parents hardly noticed when I got up from the table, scraped my cold General Tso's into the sink, and headed upstairs, where at least my anxiety could consume me in private.

I had to hand it to her; Mary Katherine's little guilt trip had been effective. Since her needling comment about Robert, the same feeling I had gotten in the pit of my stomach when Jamie told me about Jake had returned. Had I unintentionally done to Mary Price what Jamie had done to me? I'd broken the cardinal rule of friendship: never, ever, under any circumstances, barring having to repopulate the earth in the event of a nuclear holocaust, go after another girl's ex. What if I had cost myself the best friend I'd made since moving to Beaufort?

After serious contemplation, I realized my only option was to call Mary Price, explain the situation, and prostrate myself at her feet. Cross-legged on my bed, I took a deep breath and punched her number on speed dial.

"Hey," she answered on the second ring. "What's goin' on?"

"Hey."

"Are you watching *Ocean Drive*? That's so eff'd up what Justin just did to Kayla."

Was that a veiled hint? "I'm not watching. Actually, there's something I wanted to ask you."

"Oh. Okay, shoot. We're on commercial break." I heard the television go mute.

"Uh, well, see . . ." I wavered before finally spitting it out like a bad piece of meat. "I was just wondering if you were upset, or mad, that I asked Robert to be my escort."

"Why would I be mad?"

"I don't know. MK seemed to think I should have asked you first. . . . You know, 'cause you and Robert used to hook up? I just didn't think about it—"

"Annie, seriously," Mary Price interrupted, "that is like old news. Like ancient old news. I *definitely* do not have feelings for Robert. Honest, he's like a brother to me. It creeps me out to even *think* I kissed him."

"Really?" I insisted. I needed to know she wasn't just saying it, being the polite Southern girl who pretends like nothing bothers her, when really she'd like to slash your tires.

"Annie, I'm glad you invited him," Mary Price assured. "I felt really bad that I couldn't, but I had to have my brother and cousin. But now Robert can come. Seriously, it's all good."

"Are you sure?" I needed to hear it again. "You're not just saying that?"

"I would tell you; I'm your friend." She was, which made me smile. "I'm totally fine with it. . . . And I bet he's more than fine with it, too," she teased. "Annie, he's like, totally in love with you."

"No he's not. . . ." *Really?!* "Oh my gosh, you have no idea how relieved I am. I've been freaking out about this all night." I flopped back on my bed, released from my guilt.

"Well, seriously, freak no more. Ooh, *Ocean*'s back on. I'll call you when it's over."

"'Kay."

I hung up and heaved a colossal sigh before padding downstairs to see what, exactly, Justin had done to Kayla.

EIGHTEEN

*A lady is never the first to arrive for,
or the last to leave, a party.*

Lanterns lined the walkway from the front-lawn-turned-parking lot to Belmont's open front door. The house was lit from the inside like a pumpkin on Halloween. There were hors d'oeuvres in the library, a bar in the drawing room, and a band out back, where strands of lights illuminated the magnolia trees like lightning bugs. As I scanned the backyard for the girls, I was stunned to think all of this was in honor of me. Well, me and my three friends. I smiled.

Out on the black-and-white-checkered dance floor, a few couples were already swaying to Motown music, but none of them included Mary Price, Taylor, Bliss (who, in the Debutante Planning Committee's infinite mercy, was allowed at the parties, if not the ball), or even Mary Katherine (who was still avoiding me). I did, however, spot Robert chatting by the chocolate fountain with two adults I didn't recognize. My stomach did the familiar somersault that signaled to the rest of my body his presence. Since Valentine's Day, there had been increasing flirtation but, to my frustration, no consummation. My psyche could not handle another shoulder hug or back pat.

It was now or never. Running my hands nervously down my sides, I shook my hair behind my shoulders and took a deep breath. Bliss had gone shopping with me for my dress. It was strapless, periwinkle, and a little shorter than I might have chosen, but Bliss had convinced me it brought out my eyes and showed off my legs. Bliss knew about these kinds of things, so I believed her, and a pre-party vanity check in my parents' full-length mirror had confirmed it: I looked hot. If Robert didn't make a move tonight, it could be for only one reason, and he certainly didn't *seem* gay.

But just as my mental entrance music started and I prepared to strut my stuff across the yard, Gram zeroed in. Suddenly I was being dragged through the party like a ventriloquist's doll, to be introduced to every person over fifty. Apparently, this wasn't just a party *for* me, it was a party *about* me, and though I was trying to be polite, every single person asked the same questions over and over—and over—again. By the fifth go-round, I had the script down pat. The conversation would begin with a comment on how pretty Belmont looked (Me: "It looks so beautiful. I've never seen it like this!") and end with a question about where I was going to school in the fall (Me: "Brown . . . Rhode Island . . . Yes, I'm very excited.").

So when Courtney appeared in front of me with an overenthused hug and a high-pitched "heyyya," I was more than slightly relieved. Unthinkingly, I returned the squeal. Even as the saccharine salutation escaped my mouth, I caught myself, appalled. I had sworn I would never emit that nausea-inducing sound. As Courtney told me how cute I looked, I regained my composure, thanked her, and tried to dismiss my temporary slip of character. It was going to be a very long night.

I finally escaped Gram's clutches under the pretense of needing to powder my nose, and immediately went in search of Mary Price, someone I wouldn't have to "heyyya" to. When I found her by the shrimp cocktail, she promptly pulled me into the drawing room to flirt with the young and only mildly attractive bartender, who in turn snuck us a couple of very strong rum and Cokes. This was a brilliant idea until, coming from the bathroom, I was intercepted by my father.

"Hey, Banannie. Enjoying the party?" he asked hopefully, twirling his Scotch.

"Yeah, it's great," I answered quickly, trying to slip out of the narrow hall before he could smell the liquor on my own breath.

"Do you want to dance? I've requested 'My Girl.'"

It was a favorite. One of my earliest memories, before we even moved to Connecticut, was of standing on my dad's feet as he danced around our tiny, New York apartment to the sounds of the Temptations.

"Sure, Dad. Later," I promised distractedly.

"All right," he answered, unable to hide his disappointment. "Well, save it for me."

As I started to go, I felt the grip of regret. But when I turned to say I'd reconsidered, it was too late; my father was already in conversation with a bald man in a yellow bow tie. Cutting through the crush of people outside— not easy at a party of more than two hundred people—I spotted Mary Price, Bliss, and Taylor laughing, across the dance floor. I snaked my way through spinning couples to join them.

"What were you laughing at?" I asked, looking in the direction of their collective gaze.

"The boys," Mary Price said, rolling her eyes. "They're shamelessly flirting with those freshmen over there."

"So predictable," Bliss added, rolling her eyes in confirmation.

Standing on my tiptoes for a better view, I peered through the crowd. To my amazement and dismay, the eyelash-batting freshmen were, in fact, Virginia and Charlotte, and they were all but throwing themselves on Robert, Ryker, and Smalley.

"Oh no," I groaned. "Those are my cousins."

The twins had certainly come a long way from the days of matching jumpers. Virginia was wearing a dress the size of a cocktail napkin, and a sliver of pink belly was just visible between Charlotte's white tube top and low-slung fuchsia skirt. What a difference a school year could make. I was surprised Gram had let them out of the house.

"Really?" Bliss asked, astonished. "They don't look like you."

"Yeah, I know." It was my turn to roll my eyes.

"Come to think of it, though, I guess my cousins don't look much like me either," Bliss said, biting pensively on the end of a cocktail straw.

As she launched into a meandering monologue, all I could focus on were the twins. My cousins were giggling with exaggerated delight at whatever James Smalley was saying. True, I had noticed his tendency to become a one-man act at parties, but *come on*, I thought. He wasn't *that* freaking funny. Smalley must have called Robert out on something, because as I watched, the latter defensively threw up his hands, and Virginia poked him in the chest in coy shock. He flashed her one of his hundred-watt smiles, and I almost vomited on my shoes.

What did these little tarts think they were doing coming to *our* party and hanging all over *our* boys? They were freshmen! These were seniors! They couldn't just waltz in here and, and, and . . . *flirt* with them. It was *my* barely-there dress Robert was supposed to be having indecent thoughts about, not Virginia's. I had half—make that three-quarters—of a mind to go over there with a bucket of cold water and break it up myself.

"Annie? Are you okay?" Bliss asked.

I snapped back to the conversation and realized my hands had somehow clenched into fists. "Sorry, what were you saying?"

"I was telling Mary Price and Taylor about the guy we met at the mall when we got your dress," Bliss said. "You thought he was cute, didn't you?"

"Oh yeah," I agreed. "Yeah, he was cute." But to be honest, I couldn't remember. My attention was stuck on Robert and the twin tartlettes.

When the band launched into the opening lines of "My Girl," I was still fuming. My father, like every other father at the party, tapped his daughter on the back. "May I have this dance?" he asked.

I nodded, and we took our place on the crowded floor. As we rocked back and forth to the familiar tune, I was discomfited by a very unwelcome sight over my dad's shoulder: Smalley was all but grinding with Charlotte. Under normal circumstances, this would have been enough to strike me temporarily blind, but at the moment, I could have cared less about Charlotte—because next to her, Robert was dancing with Virginia. As my father and I spun across the dance floor, I tried to position us so I could keep an eye on them. Were they talking? Was he smiling? *How low was his hand on her back?* And, most important, how, with the party almost halfway over, had my escort still failed to notice me wearing a dress that deserved noticing?

When the song ended—what seemed like an eternity later—my dad thanked me for the dance. Distracted, I smiled, hugged him, and then quickly headed toward the area where Virginia and Robert had been. All I found were Ryker and Smalley.

"Hey, great party, Annie," said Ryker. "Your grand-parents' house is awesome. It's like an old plantation."

"Yeah, it *is* an old plantation." I didn't have the patience for this. "Listen, have you guys seen Robert?"

"He's somewhere with that freshman. I think he took her to the woods." Smalley crunched casually on ice from his drink.

Ouch. "Oh." My cheeks burned.

"Hey, I got a flask in my pocket," Smalley said furtively. "You want a pull?" He sounded like one of those street-corner drug pushers with a flattop and bad teeth you see in health class videos.

I considered for a moment. Yes I did.

We moved out of the light and turned our backs to the

crowd. Smalley took a small, monogrammed silver flask from his jacket pocket. Unscrewing the top, he glanced once more around before handing it to me. Tilting the flask back, I took two long swigs, nearly choking on the strong liquid that stung my nose and throat as it burned its way down to my stomach. Immediately I knew it had been a bad idea.

"Thanks," I wheezed, wiping my mouth with the back of my hand. Then, spotting the Marys, Taylor, and Bliss on the back steps, I quickly excused myself. "I'm gonna find the girls. I'll see ya later."

My disgust at both Robert and the whiskey must have been written on my face, because as I walked up, I was greeted with a tactful, "Whoa, what's wrong with you?" from Mary Katherine. They were the first words she had said to me all evening. Apparently Mary Katherine was willing to "talk" to me if it meant insulting me in some way.

"My escort's disappeared with my fourteen-year-old cousin," I said with the colorless tone of a news anchor.

"That's why you're not supposed to ask your boyfriend to be your escort," she said bluntly. "If you break up or get in a fight or something, things get really awkward."

I stared at Mary Katherine for a long second, suppressing the primal impulse to smack her in her smug little face.

"Well, Robert's not my boyfriend," I snapped, no longer making any effort to conceal the aggravation in my voice. "And we're not in a fight."

"All I'm saying is one year there was a huge scene when this girl and her escort broke up at the ball 'cause—"

"I know!" I cut her off. "He cheated on her. Jeez, God forbid someone make a scene at the *Magnolia Ball*."

"Well, I mean, the whole freaking town's there."

"Not the whole town," reminded Bliss quietly.

"What is it with *you people* and this stupid debutante ball?" I lashed out with an animosity that surprised even me. All the warm feelings I'd developed for Beaufort in the past few months had apparently dissolved in those pulls of whiskey. "You make it this exclusive thing, where you have all these picky little rules just to make it seem proper or something. . . ." I didn't realize I was raising my voice. ". . . And you all take it so seriously, like it's the end-all-be-all of your perfect, little, Southern existence."

With these last words, something broke. Before I knew it, hot tears streamed down my face. People around me turned, craning their necks to see who was shouting. Mary Price put her hand on my shoulder.

"Annie, it's okay," she said softly, glancing at Taylor and Bliss, who were equally stunned. "Come on, let's go to the bathroom."

She grabbed me by the hand and started to weave

through the crowd, pulling me behind her. At the door of the house, we met my mother. "Annie, are you okay?" she asked, alarmed.

I was crying too hard to answer. She looked at Mary Price, who shook her head to say she hadn't the slightest idea either.

"Come on, honey," my mother said, taking me by the shoulders. "Do you want to go home?"

"Yes!" I croaked. "I want to go *home*! To Connecticut! I hate this stupid town, and I hate this stupid excuse for a bunch of stupid parties! *I* am not a debutante! I can't be!" I erupted into more tears, shaking under the emotional weight.

"Shhhh," my mother soothed, stroking my hair. She put her arm around me and I surrendered, nestling my head into her chest. "Thanks, Mary Price," she said. "I'm gonna take Annie upstairs."

"Sure, Mrs. MacRae. Annie, I'm sorry," Mary Price whispered, but she sounded as if she didn't quite know what she was apologizing for. "Call me tomorrow."

I let my mother lead me up the creaky back stairs to Gram's bathroom. It smelled like my grandmother: an oddly comforting combination of talcum powder and White Shoulders perfume. My mom sat me on the toilet and crouched so that our faces were level. Rolling a wad of toilet paper around her hand, she handed it to me. I blew my nose but continued to sob uncontrollably, the tears coming despite squeezing my eyes so tight that I could see red shapes against my black eyelids.

Not saying a word, she pulled my head into her chest, enfolding me in her arms and in her own familiar scent. Like when I was little and woke up from a bad dream, she slowly rocked me from side to side. I let her hold me until the crying subsided and I quieted, swollen and red-eyed.

Finally she pulled away and looked at me. The look on her face wasn't angry or even confused. It was sympathetic. "You weren't having fun?" she asked gently.

"I am," I squeaked, "but I don't *want* to. I'm not supposed to. This wasn't supposed to happen. Don't you understand?"

Pulling back, I waited. I needed her to understand, because at that moment I wasn't sure I even did.

NINETEEN

A lady can give and accept an apology.

I opened one eye. My head was pounding, my stomach was queasy, and my mouth felt like it was stuffed with cotton. I'd had a horrible dream. Oh God, it flashed through my head, it wasn't a dream! The memory of the night before came rushing back to me like a train hurtling toward a horrific wreck. Scenes from the night before popped like one of my mother's flashbulbs in my mind. My mom in the bathroom. Virginia and Robert. My public freak-out. I cringed. The whiskey. Oh gross, the whiskey. Groaning, I pulled the covers over my head, as if they could keep out the events of the previous night, and drifted back into a fitful sleep.

When I woke again, it was almost two in the afternoon. A glass of water and two Extra Strength Tylenol had mysteriously appeared on my bedside table. I took them, not wanting to think about who'd put them there. My headache was gone, but my moral hangover wasn't. I propped myself up on one elbow and grabbed my phone. Six missed calls: Mary Price, Bliss, Taylor, Mary Price, a number I didn't recognize, and Mary Katherine. With dread, I dialed my voice mail.

"Hey," Mary Price's voice came through the phone. "Just wanted to check on you. Give me a call when you get up."

Bliss's and Taylor's messages said virtually the same thing. I felt horrible. Hideous. Horrendous. Ghastly. Every nasty word in the dictionary. I had publicly insulted not just their town and the debutante tradition but, by proxy, them, my supposed friends, and they were the ones calling to console *me*?

"Hey. It's me again. Worried about you. Call me," entreated Mary Price's second message. I took a sip of water.

"Hey, Annie. It's Robert. Just wonderin' where you went off to last night. Mary Price said you went home early. Hope you're feelin' okay. Had fun. It was a great party. Give me a call."

Where did *I* go off to? Had fun? It was a great party? The nerve! I listened to the message three times, then erased it with disgust.

"Hey, Annie. It's MK. Look, I don't really know what happened last night, but I think maybe we should talk. Give me a call. Okay, talk to you later."

As I flipped the phone shut, my door creaked open and my mother appeared. "How ya feeling?" she asked, leaning in the doorway, arms crossed over her chest. Some of the previous night's sympathy had turned to "I told you so."

"Not so great," I admitted, rolling over on my back.

"Thought that might be the case. Do you need anything?"

"To be put out of my misery. Can I just have some time to recover before I'm punished?"

"We're going to a movie, but we'll be back in a couple of hours. Come down then."

"Thanks."

She closed the door. It was time for damage control, and I figured I might as well get the worst over with first. I dialed Mary Katherine's number.

"Hey," she answered briskly.

"Hey," I said, gulping down a sour wave of nausea. "I'm really sorry about last night." Why beat around the bush? "I don't know why I freaked out. I've just been stressed. Moving down here was hard, then with college and Jake and Jamie, and you've been sort of weird, and then all the deb stuff. . . . I don't know, it just came to a head last night. I didn't mean to go ballistic. I didn't even mean most of what I said."

"No, I should apologize, too. I guess I just got jealous of the new girl."

"Jealous? Why would you possibly be jealous of *me*?" It was an absurd thought that my alcohol-logged brain could not comprehend. I was the wreck, the fish out of water flopping around trying to find the pond she belonged in.

"I don't know," Mary Katherine confessed. "Everyone likes you, and the guys think you're hot, and you and Mary Price were hanging out all the time. . . ."

This was all news to me.

"Anyway," she continued, "I'm sorry. I realize I've been a real bitch lately."

She was sincere, I could tell; and if I had learned anything, it was that apologies did not come easily for Mary Katherine.

"Yeah," I conceded with a laugh, "you have been."

"Thanks! You're supposed to say, 'No, Mary Katherine, you could never be a bitch!'"

"But that's why we love you," I assured.

"I know, I know."

"Seriously, though, I had no idea you felt that way. You should have said something."

"Well, I'm kind of shy," she joked, at which I had to laugh. "So we're okay then? You're not mad at me?"

"No. And you're not mad at me?"

"Water under the bridge."

"Cool."

"How are you feeling, by the way?"

"Better."

It was a long afternoon seeking pardons for my impromptu tirade. Amazingly, no one seemed to hold it against me. They said it was fine, they understood. Mary Price even told me about a meltdown she'd had at a party last year when she and Dalton were breaking up. "*Ten* times worse than yours," she assured me.

Too soon, though, it was time to face the music with my parents. I'd heard them return from the movies, but afraid the smell of food might send me lurching toward the bathroom, I waited till they were done with dinner to come downstairs. I was hoping they wouldn't ground me, although on second thought, sometimes grounding was preferable to my father's "talks."

Reluctantly, I slipped on my robe and slippers and ventured to the living room. My father was planted on the couch, feet propped on a stool, one hand holding a beer and the other buried in a bowl of pretzels by his side. My mother wasn't around.

"Hey," I said sheepishly.

"Ah, she rouses. How are you feeling?" he asked, raising his eyebrows in paternal know-it-allness.

"Okay. What are you watching?" I asked, hoping maybe to distract him with small talk.

"Basketball."

"I thought basketball season was over."

"It's an old Carolina game. Your dad's finally discovering the glories of cable. Did you know we have over five hundred channels?"

With the exception of the news and the occasional History Channel documentary, my father *never* watched television. That he was vegging in front of it now made me fear I'd finally succeeded in driving him to the brink. Next thing I knew, we'd be getting twenty-thousand-dollar credit card bills from the Home Shopping Network.

"ESPN Classics," he explained, pointing with the remote at the glowing screen. "I think this may be my new addiction."

"Replacing that crack habit?" I joked lightheartedly.

"Exactly." He patted the couch next to him. "Why don't you join me?"

I was most definitely *not* in the mood to watch men in short-shorts and Afros run up and down a basketball court, but I doubted I had much say at the moment, so obediently I curled into a ball at the end of the sofa. I eyed my father suspiciously. Was this to be part of my punishment?

"So . . ." he sighed.

Here it comes . . .

". . . what happened last night?"

"I just got upset," I mumbled, staring down at my ragged cuticles and chipped nails.

"Would you like to share why?" he asked, lowering the volume on the television.

"Dad," I began, then stopped. "Are you happy here?"

He was silent, thoughtful, for a moment. I could hear the muted chatter of the sports announcers on TV.

"Yes," he said, nodding slowly. "I think I am."

"You *think* you are?"

"Well, Annie, I've found happiness is a hard state to pin down. There are always things we like and dislike about any situation. But am I glad we moved down here? *Yes*, I'd say that I am."

"So why did you leave in the first place?"

The leather couch squeaked as he readjusted to look me earnestly in the eyes.

"Oh no," I whimpered. "Dad, we don't have to have a father-daughter moment. I'll just take the lecture."

"No, I'm glad you brought it up. I want to explain something to you."

"Cue cheesy, swelling background music," I sighed.

He ignored my sarcastic attempt to derail his little heart-to-heart, and continued. "There were a lot of expectations on me growing up, Annie." He shook his head heavily. "And I always did the things expected of me. But one day I realized I was living the life everyone *else* wanted for me. I hadn't even thought about what *I* wanted because my life was already laid out."

"Didn't that make you mad?" I wondered, thinking how supremely it pissed me off having Gram plot my debut, let alone how I would have felt had it been my life.

"Yes and no. My life was comfortable, but I started feeling like a cookie cutter. I figured there was more to the world, and to *me*, than Beaufort could show me. So I took a chance and left pretty much everything I knew behind."

"And you met Mom and had me."

"Yep." He nodded. "And we made the decision to stay up North, which, as you can imagine, was not a popular decision with Gram." He sipped his beer and smiled matter-of-factly at me.

"But if you liked Connecticut, why didn't we just stay there?" I was confused.

"I did like Connecticut, but you know, I realized something else, also. I thought I was running away from something in Beaufort, but I ran right back into it up there. I thought Beaufort was small and closed-minded, too obsessed with surface and civility . . . then I realized I knew as many people who didn't know their head from their ass in Connecticut as I did back in Beaufort."

"So that's why you moved back?"

"Well, that and the job offer . . . and I missed it. I realized I rather like Beaufort."

We both sat in silence as the UNC Tar Heels's 1979 victory against NC State went unnoticed on the television.

"It doesn't matter where you are. Your world's as big as you make it," my dad finally said, emphasizing each word by jabbing the air with his beer bottle. "Does that make any sense?"

"Sort of," I answered.

"It will."

"Is our *Full House* moment over now?"

"Whatever that means, yes, our 'moment' is over. You're dismissed." He raised the volume on the television again and grabbed a handful of pretzels. "That was a great game," he mused, more to himself than to me.

Suddenly I remembered something my foggy brain had been trying to repress. Turning at the foot of the stairs, I proceeded cautiously, "Um, did Gram, uh, you know . . ."

After the previous night's performance, I would have been surprised if she hadn't disowned me. And although that might have been an answer to our problems, it was not, for various reasons, the ideal one.

"She called," my dad said quietly. "You might want to include an apology when you send your thank-you note for the party."

"Consider it done," I pledged, and plodded back to bed. I could only hope that my presence at the ball would eclipse my blowup. But I was pretty sure Gram would not let me forget it . . . ever.

* * *

Tramping behind Mary Price and Mary Katherine across the wet athletic field, I jumped over puddles and laughed as my flip-flops made obscene sucking noises in the fresh mud. With my temper tantrum forgiven if not forgotten and only a week of classes left before graduation, we were all in a good mood as we approached the clump of sherbet-colored polos and khakis on the sidelines.

Country Day's boys' lacrosse team was staggeringly bad, to the point of masochism. Their season had involved humiliations piled on top of losses. Nevertheless (or maybe because of this), the seniors had come out en masse to cheer their classmates through their final high school game. Queasily, I picked Robert out among them. The only acceptable course of action was, of course, to ignore him, as I had been trying to do since the party last weekend.

The girls had left the boys to mill around on the soggy sidelines and were perched on raincoats spread across the bleachers, still beaded with rain from the recent spring showers.

"Did Ryker start this quarter?" Mary Katherine asked, plopping down on a blue raincoat next to Bliss.

"Yep," Bliss replied, claiming her grape Slurpee from my hand.

Bored at the beating the lacrosse team was taking, we had volunteered for a fourth-quarter Slurpee run.

"He is so weird," Mary Katherine grumbled. "He

insists that I come to these things, even though they get their butts kicked every time."

"Awww. He just wants to show off his manliness by chasing other boys around and beating them with sticks," Mary Price teased, tearing open a pack of Twizzlers and offering them down the line.

"Seriously," Mary Katherine agreed, gnawing off a piece of the rubbery, red stick.

As expected, BCD, despite a valiant effort, lost five to one. The exhausted, mud-caked players trooped off the field, giving each other halfhearted respect knuckles. We came off the bleachers to greet them, and instantly Ryker's gloomy attitude changed. He grabbed Mary Katherine and lifted her in a bear hug. "Hey, babe!"

She squirmed. "Ryker, you're all sweaty and muddy! Put me down!"

"You like my man scent," he teased, returning her to the ground.

"Gross," she squealed, weakly shoving him away.

Mary Price and I exchanged a nauseated look. We were all used to Mary Katherine and Ryker's penchant for PDA, but that didn't mean we had to enjoy it.

"Hey, y'all." Robert casually appeared at my side.

"Hey," Mary Price said tentatively, glancing at me for my reaction. I had told her about Robert and Virginia, and then some. As all good girlfriends would, she'd spent a considerable amount of time dissecting the situation from every possible angle with me. Which meant she was as aware as I of the intense awkwardness this moment was creating.

"I'm gonna go to the bathroom," I said pointedly to her, making clear to Robert that I chose to neither see nor hear him. "I'll meet you by the car in a few."

With that slap in the face firmly executed, I turned on my heel and started for the field house. I was almost to the squat brick building when I heard squishy, quick footsteps behind me. Robert jogged up, falling in step beside me.

"Hey," he attempted.

"Hey," I said, refusing to look at him.

"Are you mad at me or something?"

"Why would I be mad at you?" I stared straight ahead and kept my pace.

"I don't know. You've been ignoring me since your party. Did I do something to piss you off?"

"You can do whatever you want."

"Annie, what's wrong?" he asked, confused.

"Look, if you want to be that creepy older guy who preys on freshmen, that's your prerogative."

"What? What are you talking about?" He furrowed his eyebrows.

"You do know Virginia's my little cousin, don't you?" I emphasized the word "little."

"The freshman at your party?" he asked, a smile of recognition playing on his mouth.

"Yeah, that one," I answered, shooting him a disgusted glare. How had I been so wrong about him? I had honestly believed he'd managed to evolve beyond single-minded slime like Jake. "The one you took to the woods, which by the way, is like, so pedophile."

Robert laughed. "Annie, stop a second. . . . Stop," he said, grabbing my wrist so that I had to turn to face him. I wriggled free. "Annie, I took Virginia to the woods because she was puking, and I didn't want her to get in trouble. Her sister was with us."

I stared over his shoulder at the lacrosse field, where Mary Price and Bliss were watching us, and weighed what he said.

"Is that also why you were dancing with her?" I scoffed, as if I had a right to the question.

"No, I was dancing with her because you were already dancing with your dad and because Smalley wanted to hook up with Charlotte," he said, stuffing his hands into his pockets and looking at me intently.

I glanced from his face to the field and back, biting my lip. Should I believe him? Could I believe him? I had naively trusted both Jake and Jamie and that hadn't worked out so hot for me.

"Look, Annie . . ." Robert examined his sneakers, as if the words he was searching for might be written on them. "I thought it was obvious . . . but I like you. *You.* Not your fourteen-year-old cousin."

"You like me?" I asked, cocking an eyebrow and restraining the excitement that was welling up in my chest. I wanted to hear him say it again.

"Yeah." He shrugged sweetly. "I like you."

I couldn't stop the smile that was spreading across my face. My heart was beating so loudly against my ribs I was sure he could hear it. "Good," I said finally. "'Cause I like you too."

We locked eyes for a century-long second, both of us smiling at the palpable promise that hung in the air, before I turned and continued walking to the field house. I let myself glance back only once. Robert was still watching me, grinning, his bright yellow shirt standing out like a sure sign against the gray sky.

TWENTY

A lady does not kiss and tell.

The flames of the bonfire carried bits of ash and glowing orange cinders into the night sky. Earlier that afternoon, our parents and classmates had cheered as we were each handed a scrolled diploma. I had thought the event signaling the end of my days at Beaufort Country Day School would be a relief, but the tears I'd dabbed at with a tissue, mercifully passed to me by Taylor, were surprisingly not tears of joy.

After the obligatory family lunches and congratulations, twenty of us had hightailed it to Mary Price's country house, which her parents had kindly agreed to let us use on the condition of "good behavior." We had cooked out, letting the boys be boys and grill hamburgers and build a bonfire in the field behind the house. A few people had pitched tents, as the house couldn't sleep us all, and Smalley had pulled his truck up to the makeshift campsite to provide music. People talked and laughed around the fire. Nostalgia was running high as everyone passed stories of their last thirteen years together. I hadn't been there thirteen months, but the memories tugged at me as if they were my own. Looking around, I marveled at the things I'd miss: MK's inappropriate jokes, Bliss's wide-eyed naiveté, Taylor's laugh and excessive punctuation—even in text messages. Mary Price. And Robert.

It was much colder here than in Beaufort, and as I watched the flames dance higher, I pulled the sweater I'd borrowed from Mary Price around myself tightly, sliding my hands up into the long sleeves.

I was acutely aware that Robert had not left my side all night. We were sitting side by side on a log as Mary Katherine regaled us with a story about a fight she and Bliss had had over Tommy Pintz in the fourth grade. MK had told Tommy that Bliss ate her boogers. When Bliss found out, she told her mother, who immediately called Mary Katherine's mother. MK had lost television privileges for a week. It had been devastating.

As we laughed, Robert put his arm around my waist. I shivered, less from the evening chill than from being so close to him; but it worked to my advantage, because he instinctively pulled me closer.

The loudening noise of an engine coming over the field caught our attention, and momentarily, Mary Price and Smalley roared up to the bonfire on a small vehicle that looked something like a cross between a tractor, a go-cart, and a dirt bike on steroids. Mary Price jumped down, her cheeks pink. "Annie, you want a ride?"

"On what? That thing?"

"*That thing* is a four-wheeler!" she said as if it were the most obvious thing in the world.

Robert turned to me. "You've never been on one?"

"No. Where I grew up, we rode in cars, not farm vehicles."

"Come on," he said, pulling me off the log. "I'll drive."

I looked at Mary Price, who shooed me toward the four-wheeler. "Go! You can take a tour of the property. It's really nice back through those trees. There's another field."

I climbed into the big, molded seat behind Robert with the same trepidation I would have had mounting a rodeo bull. Robert squeezed a lever on the handlebars, and the four-wheeler lurched forward. I nearly toppled off the back, grabbing a fistful of shirt.

"Whoa there, cowboy!" I shouted into his ear over the chainsaw drone of the engine. "You sure you know how to drive this thing?"

I wrapped my arms around his waist, able to see just the edge of his smile as he guided us up into the dark field. We bumped over rocks and sliced through the tall grass. Chilled by the wind whipping past us, I nestled my face into his fleece, my eyes peeking over his shoulder.

He smelled like wood smoke from the bonfire.

Robert slowed at the tree line, expertly maneuvering the bulky vehicle around trees and boulders. When we came out on the other side, it was beautiful. The light from the house and the bonfire was blocked out by the trees, and in the darkness above us, the sky was full of stars. I couldn't remember the last time I'd seen so many.

Robert did a lap around the empty land. I closed my eyes and bounced along, content, until he drove into the center of the field and turned off the engine. Opening my eyes, I tilted back my head and took in the sky.

"It's pretty, huh?" he asked.

I nodded in agreement, too tongue-tied to speak. My heart rattled my rib cage. This was when people kissed—when it was too romantic to do anything but gaze lovingly into each other's eyes and take someone in a passionate embrace as the background music swelled. I wanted Robert to kiss me, but I wasn't used to romantic embraces. I was better at nervous, slightly awkward embraces. After all, that's what first kisses were really like, not the staged crap you saw in the movies.

But it seemed Robert wasn't here for kissing. He dismounted and stood by the four-wheeler, his hands shoved into the pockets of his Carhartts and his head thrown back. "I used to love going up to the mountains. My dad would bring me to this tiny, little cabin for the opening of hunting season. It was a shack, really. We'd sleep on these lumpy cots in our sleeping bags and cook with a camping stove and wake up when it was still dark."

He smiled down at me, still sitting on the back of the four-wheeler.

"Do you miss him?" I asked.

"Yeah. But it's funny, sometimes I still feel like he's here." He kicked at the grass with his toe.

I nodded, looking up at his face framed in a blanket of stars. Then he did something that felt so natural it took me by surprise: he leaned over and kissed me. And it was sweet and perfect—*exactly* like you see in the movies.

Robert pulled me from the four-wheeler and wrapped his arms around me. He was warm. With my arms around his neck, I leaned into him and let go, kissing him like I'd wanted to since the day he showed me to Mr. Smith's English class.

Suddenly I opened my eyes and stopped. Strains of music were drifting through the trees.

"Do you hear that?" I asked, pulling away without letting go.

Robert listened. "Oh no," he said, a tiny smile playing at the edges of his mouth as the music grew louder.

Whoever was controlling the truck radio had pumped it to full volume, and I could just make out the song. I cocked my head to listen. "Did I hear that correctly?"

Robert lowered his head, hiding a smile. "Yes," he acknowledged shamefully. "You can thank Smalley. . . . At least it isn't 'Honky Tonk Badonkadonk.'"

I busted out laughing. "Seriously? 'She Thinks My Tractor's Sexy'?"

"Yes," he confirmed.

"Well." I grinned. "Maybe she does."

I know a lady doesn't kiss and tell, but by the time we finally returned to the campfire, I didn't have to—my smile said it all.

TWENTY-ONE

A lady knows how to dance.

It was starting to get hot, but as they said in these parts, it wasn't the heat, it was the humidity that was getting to me. It was so oppressive, in fact, I had sought refuge in our claw-foot, upstairs bathtub—the perfect spot for a refreshing bubble bath on a summer evening. Soaking in the suds, I dangled my hands over the sides to avoid pruning. A single drop of water trickled down my index finger and dripped onto the sheet of paper lying on the floor next to the tub.

The copy of my Brown application essay had been sandwiched between chapters five and six of my calculus textbook. It had floated down from the pages, landing at my feet in the textbook return line at BCD's bookstore. Preoccupied with deb duties and graduation fêtes, the two carefully typewritten pages had lain unnoticed on the desk in my bedroom until this afternoon, when they resurfaced as I searched for my monogrammed stationery, on which I was expected to write Gram a thank-you note for the pearl earrings she had given me as a graduation present. (The note accompanying the earrings had "suggested" I wear them at the deb ball.)

I had brought the essay with me for some bath-time reading. Leaning over the tub, I picked it up, trying not to wet the pages. The question I had chosen had been eerily pertinent: Discuss an experience in your life that has led to significant (positive or negative) change. Ha.

"From almost the day we are born," I now read, "we are told that change is good, change is inevitable. We are told that to move forward in life, we must take steps—in the beginning baby ones, and as we grow older, ever-greater symbolic strides toward self-actualization and improvement."

SAT word, ten points, I thought. The overblown prose was almost laughable to me now. How, I wondered, had I been so lucky as to convince the Brown admissions board with this pretentious hooey?

"For, as Mr. Darwin taught us," I continued reading, "survival requires adaptation."

The bathroom was steamy, and beads of sweat were collecting on my lip and forehead. I cracked open the window by the tub, and the smell of hamburgers on the grill wafted up through the screen. I heard a distinct sizzle as my father flipped each burger and, behind that, the crickets that had once kept me up at night but whose high-pitched, rhythmic screeching was now part of the soundtrack of my life.

I turned back to the essay: "I am the first to admit that I am not a girl who likes change." I laughed out loud at the understatement of the decade. I had disliked change like I disliked shark attacks—I hated it, was terrified of it. Was it possible, though, that in just over a year even my position on change had changed?

Lolling my head back, I closed my eyes. Scenes from the past year played before me like a slide show—the long car ride from Connecticut, my first day of school, hockey, Jamie, Jake, Brown, Robert . . . and who could forget (I wished) the meetings, luncheons, dress-fittings, parties—ugh, my party. I sank below the water and came back up, wiping off the memory of that night like so many water droplets, my thoughts once again focused on the more immediate.

Every afternoon that week had been occupied by mindless rehearsals of the figure (or as Mrs. Patterson called it, "tha figyuh")—the curving arcs and circles and figure eights the debs had to gracefully trace across the parquet dance floor. There was no way, I realized, I'd ever have gotten through *any* of it without Mary Price, MK, Taylor, and even Bliss. There was a time in the not-so-distant past I wouldn't have admitted it, but there was nothing to bring you closer to a group of girls than hours of shared physical, mental, and emotional torture at the hands of a debutante committee.

I was grateful to the girls. More than grateful. Whether they knew it or not, they had pulled me through when I wanted nothing more than to dig my heels into the ground. They had suffered through and let me in—something I had needed without knowing it.

A screen door opened below, and I heard my mother's voice. It was muffled but followed by a clear laugh. I could picture her, a glass of wine in her hand, wrapping her long arm around my father's waist as he wielded the spatula with pride—Mr. Mom cooking his family dinner. With a feeling of great contentment, I realized, sitting in a lukewarm bath in the sweltering Alabama heat, that my essay no longer held true. Change had been *exactly* what I'd needed.

When I shuffled into the kitchen after my bath, a towel piled on top of my head, I found my mother standing at the kitchen counter, her back jerking as she furiously stirred something in a big, blue bowl. Odder yet, she was making a strange sound.

"Are you humming?" I asked, plucking a pickle off a plate on the table and popping it in my mouth. "When's dinner gonna be ready?" All those hamburger smells had made me hungry.

My mom spun around, her hands covered in flour.

"What are you doing?" I gasped, as if she'd turned

covered in blood rather than flour. High on the list of things that *did* not happen in the MacRae household: my mother baking.

"I'm putting the top on the apple crumble."

"Apple crumble?"

"Apple crumble."

"Okay, you're freaking me out," I said, eyeing my mother suspiciously. "Who replaced my mom with a Stepford Wife?"

"What? I'm not allowed to make a little something nice for my family?" She smiled. "Okay, you got me. It's sort of a special occasion. I've got some good news."

"Tell me it's not that little brother I used to ask for," I replied, pouring myself a glass of soy milk.

"Funny. I'll take that as a compliment." She brushed back a wisp of hair with her wrist, smudging a white line of flour across her forehead. "I was gonna tell you at dinner, but since you're sleuthing around . . . I got approached by a gallery!"

"An art gallery?"

"No, a shooting gallery." She shot me a sarcastic smile. "Yes! I sent my portfolio out when we first got here, and a gallery downtown wants me to do a show."

"That's great, Mom!" I said, patting her on the back and peering over her shoulder at the brown, clumpy mixture.

"Well"—she shrugged—"it's no MoMA, but I think

it'll be a good chance to get my name out there. The art scene in New York was just so competitive."

"Really, Mom, that's awesome. I'm proud of you. You're going to be a world-famous photographer *and* a country club mom."

"Oh, this coming from the debutante?" she joked.

"Damn straight," I said, slumping in a very unlady-like way on the counter.

"So, you ready?"

"That remains to be seen," I sighed. "Learned how to curtsy this week."

"Yeah? Let's see what ya got."

I laughed.

"Seriously, let's see it," she dared, sprinkling flour on the floor.

"All right," I conceded. I walked to the center of the kitchen, tossing my towel on the back of a chair. "Our instructor, Wayne—he's a dance teacher—he has this really bad lisp and does this thing where he holds the microphone right up to his mouth like he's gonna eat it—anyway, he's very specific. So let me make sure I get this right. I have to do Wayne justice."

I held my hand in a fist up to my face. "Ladieth, thith should be one fluid motion—gratheful *and*, if done correctly, *very* theductive." I shrugged my eyebrows sug-gestively.

"Be dethithive in your movementh . . . Don't hurry!

For goodneth thakes, girlth, thand up thraight! No one lookth gratheful with their back all hunched over like Quathimodo. . . . Ugh," I said in mock exasperation, snapping my fingers like Wayne. "Watch me!"

Pinching the sides of my terry-cloth bathrobe, I stood up straight. I pointed my foot and slid it on the ground in front of me, so that the toe barely grazed the floor. Deliberately, I circled it behind me like a compass. I bent slowly, first at the knees and then at the waist, until I was almost parallel with the kitchen floor. As I hovered in this awkward position, the screen door slid open, and I heard my father burst into laughter behind me.

"Excuse me, I think I must have walked into the wrong house. The apple crumble can't be that good!"

"Shhh! Annie's showing me her curtsy!" my mom cried between gasps of hysterical laughter. "Well done, honey. I knew we'd raised you right."

"This is what I've been reduced to, Dad," I said as I unfolded from my curtsy. "Proud?"

"As a matter of fact, yes. You're going to be a *mah-velous* debutante, my dear. Shall we practice our waltz as well?"

Without waiting for a reply, he swept me up in one grandiose motion, my left hand on his shoulder and my right holding his out by our sides, just as we'd both been taught in one of many dance classes. He twirled me in step around the kitchen, then dipped me dramatically, so that my wet hair grazed the floor.

"Wait! Let me get my camera," my mom shouted as she ran into the living room.

"I think we'll marry you off yet," my father joked, kissing me on the cheek before raising me back up. I playfully slapped him on the shoulder.

"Do that again!" my mother called as she rushed back in, camera in hand.

"No!" I cried. "Show's over. I have to get dressed; Mary Price is picking me up after dinner. You'll get the full show soon enough."

TWENTY-TWO

A lady is composed under pressure.

"Dad," I yelled down the stairs, "could they maybe be in the attic?"

"No, I definitely remember your mother putting them down here."

My father's muffled voice came from inside the hall closet. All I could see from the top of the stairs was a khaki rear end rummaging through shoe boxes of knick-knacks broken in the move, useless winter parkas once indispensable in Connecticut and now collecting dust, and other assorted junk that had accumulated in the closet over the past year.

It was almost Go Time—T minus four hours and counting until I, along with nineteen other debutantes, would float onto the dance floor and into the ranks of Beaufort society. And I couldn't find my gloves.

So far the day had been nothing short of a nightmare, beginning with an eight o'clock wake-up call so I could get to Frederick's Hair Design in time for my mani-pedi and blow-out, courtesy of who else but Aunt Nonny. I was aware that a spa day would probably be every other red-blooded American girl's dream, but all the poking and prodding and touching and fussing made me about as relaxed as a chimp in a laboratory. Adding to my anxiety, Courtney had also booked Frederick and had not understood that I wasn't so much reading the three-year-old back issue of *CosmoGIRL!* as hiding behind it. Luckily, her incessant chattering had been drowned out by the buzz of hair dryers.

Now the only thing my French-manicured hands were missing were my long, white gloves to cover them. Every debutante had to wear them, and Gram had insisted I use her old opera ones. Despite my hesitation at wearing Gram hand-me-downs, they were beautiful—past the elbow, buttery soft white leather, with mother-of-pearl buttons—and much more attractive than the cheap, stretchy satin ones I'd almost bought (and at the moment was wishing I had for backup). My father and I had been searching for almost an hour.

My mother, who'd had to join the other moms at the Club to assist with last-minute decorations, was no help. A frantic phone call relaying the mystery of the missing gloves had yielded only her stubborn insistence that she had put them in the hall closet for safe keeping. Too safe, it seemed.

I was about to yank down the creaky, dust-covered

ladder to the attic when I heard my father bellow, "Got 'em!" from downstairs.

"Where were they?" I gasped, racing to retrieve them.

He stood, holding his back. "Whew," he winced. "In a box of photographs in the back corner of the closet. Logical place."

I grabbed the gloves from his hands and vaulted back up the stairs. I had to be at the Club in thirty minutes and still hadn't done my makeup.

"You're welcome!" my father shouted behind me.

"Thank you!" I called over my shoulder.

At that moment, my mother burst through the front door. "Find 'em?" she asked breathlessly.

"Yep."

"Where were they?"

"In the closet."

I knew she was giving him her "I told you so" look. "I've got to get ready," she said. "Totty Patterson had me on moss duty, and it took forever."

Moss duty? I wondered but didn't have time to ask.

My mom peeked her head into my bathroom, giving me a quick peck on the forehead and a "hey, hon" before disappearing again.

My right eye was half lined—Mary Price had shown me how to use eyeliner without looking like a streetwalker—when I heard the phone ring. With a brush soaked in jet-black liquid poised in front of my eye, I decided to let my dad get it.

"Hi, Nonny," I heard him say from the phone in my parents' bedroom. "Getting ready. We have to have the Lady of the Hour at the Club in thirty minutes. . . . Wait, Nonny, slow down. What's the problem . . . ? Calm down and we'll figure it out. If he can't get in touch with them to pick it up, then I'm sure someone has a tux he can borrow. . . . Well, maybe someone owns tails. . . ."

I dropped my liner and appeared at their door. "What's the matter?" I mouthed.

My father held up his finger, signaling me to hang on. He was trying to speak, but Aunt Nonny wouldn't let him. I could hear her yapping excitedly on the other end.

"Nonny, just take a deep breath," he said. "This is not a crisis. Joe Russo owns the shop, right? Just give him a call at home, and see if he can meet Richard at the store. I gotta finish getting dressed. . . . Okay, you have my cell phone number. . . . Okay. Bye."

"What's the crisis?" my mother asked, stepping out of the steaming bathroom in her robe.

"Seems your cousin forgot to pick up his tails from the rental place," he told me.

"Richard!" I threw my hands in the air, completely exasperated by what already felt like the longest day of my life.

"It's fine. He'll get them," my father assured me. "He still has time. *You*," he said, turning me by the shoulders and directing me out the door, "finish getting ready. *You*"—he pointed at my mom—"get dressed. Unless you plan on wearing that."

The debutante committee was bustling but pleased; in nothing short of a miracle, there were twenty debutantes, twenty fathers, and forty escorts (all in tails) gathered for photographs in the ballroom. Everything was running like clockwork, with the minor exception that it was hot—not just "Golly, it sure is hot outside today" hot, but "If I'm not packed on ice like a transplant organ right this moment, I'll faint" hot. Even the air-conditioning was futile, since the room's huge French doors were opened out onto the patio. The girls were waving straw fans provided by the deb committee (who had learned even the prettiest debutante ain't so pretty when she's sweating like a pig).

The Club looked amazing. The columned façade of the big, white building already bore a striking resemblance to Tara, but the vintage buggy with two live horses parked on the lawn put it over the top. Inside the foyer stood two full-size cutouts of Rhett Butler and Scarlett O'Hara and a copy of the original movie poster.

In the ballroom, papier-mâché oak trees were abundantly draped in Spanish moss, and blown-up movie stills hung on the walls—a dashing Rhett embracing a fiery Scarlett, Mammy yanking Scarlett into a bone-crunching corset, a starving Scarlett digging desperately in the dirt for a radish.

The patio, where real trees had been draped with yet more moss and hundreds of twinkling lights, was reserved as a dining area. Dozens of round tables were topped with magnolia centerpieces that emitted an intoxicating smell. Even I had to admit the grand effect was magical.

I would have liked to look around more, but I was on deb duty, and there is no rest for a lady. Every debutante was expected to pose for formal photos in front of the ballroom's huge marble mantelpiece. First a solo shot, then the debutante with her escorts, with her parents, with each parent separately, with the entire family, with parents and escorts. . . . It was exhausting, the seemingly endless combinations.

Waiting in line for my photo shoot, my hands were starting to feel slightly slimy in the kid gloves. As I uselessly fanned my face with warm air, I decided whoever dreamed up the idea of above-the-elbow gloves in the deep South in mid-July deserved to be summarily shot. I saw Robert wipe a trickle of sweat from his temple with a small, white handkerchief he took from his pocket. I smiled. It was cute he kept a hankie—much cuter, and more debonair, than the snotty bandannas Jake and his crew had carried around in Connecticut. He looked damn good in a tux, too.

Finally my turn came. I tried to hold out my arms so they'd look skinnier, like Taylor had taught me, and hoped that the perspiration forming on the small of my back wasn't creating an attractive, yellow sweat stain on my dress.

With much prodding from Mary Price, I'd had a dress made almost identical to the one at Lady Slipper—a compromise between my love of the insanely expensive gown and the guilt I would have felt at spending the equivalent of a small country's gross domestic product on a dress I'd wear exactly once. It was perfect. When I'd looked in the mirror earlier in the evening, I'd surprised even myself. Whether or not I felt like a debutante, I'd at least look the part in photos.

Robert and Richard flanked me for the escort picture. Almost imperceptibly, I found myself leaning closer toward Robert. It was he, after all, I'd be kissing that night. We smiled.

Once the photo session had concluded and the next deb was under the lights, my mother tapped me on the arm. "Why don't we go outside, and you can let me take some?"

"Mommm," I groaned.

I was used to this drill. My whole life had been spent in front of my mother's camera. It was like being stalked by paparazzi in my own home.

"Come on, Annie," she pleaded. "This only happens once. Don't you want photographic proof?"

"Honestly? No."

She looked at me beseechingly.

"Fine," I agreed, following her out to the patio and patiently allowing myself to be positioned, fluffed, and posed. My mom liked to talk to her subjects as she worked. She said it kept them "at ease."

"You seem to be hanging in there pretty well," she said, squinting from behind the camera. *Click*.

"Yeah," I sighed, "I have to admit . . ." *Click* ". . . and this is strictly between you and me" . . . *Click, click* "mother-daughter confidentiality and all . . ." *Click* "but maybe it's not *as* bad as I thought."

She paused, lowering her camera as if she was absorbing what I'd said, then squatted down again, raising the viewfinder to her eye. *Click*.

"Mom, that's a horrible angle! You're gonna give me a double chin!"

"Hey, you do your job; I'll do mine." She stood. "So you're enjoying yourself?" she asked hopefully.

"I don't know if I'd say *enjoying* myself. I still feel like an imposter, you know? This isn't me."

"You seem to have a lot of ideas about who you aren't, Annie." My mom dropped the camera around her neck and planted herself on the brick ledge beside me.

"Everyone feels like an imposter sometimes. That's life. This probably isn't the last time you'll find yourself playing a role you wouldn't have picked for yourself, but it doesn't change who you are. It's just the part you've been cast in for the time being."

"'All the world's a stage, and all the men and women merely players,'" I quoted, staring off into the distance at a father and young son practicing on the putting green. We'd studied *As You Like It* in Mr. Smith's class. For some reason, this line had stuck with me.

"Kind of," she said.

We watched the son sink a putt and his father give him a congratulatory pat on the back.

"I mean that no one can define *you* for you, Annie. No matter what you do, where you go, or what roles you find yourself playing, who you are is deeper than that, and all these exterior things can't change it. You are who you are."

I smiled. "Did you and Dad have to go to school to learn these speeches, like Child Rearing 101?" My mom started to object. "I'm kidding! I know . . . I just don't want to be fake."

"You've never been fake, Annie," she said quietly. "Never."

I hoped mom was right. We sat in silence for a few moments until finally she stood. "Shall we go?" she asked.

I sighed. "Yeah, I guess we shall."

As we started back toward the ballroom, I remembered something. My photo with Henry at the hospital hadn't made it into the newspaper.

"Mom, will you make an extra print of one of those for me? I have a friend I want to send it to."

Back in the ballroom, Totty Patterson was trying, not very successfully, to get the attention of the debs and their escorts, who were scattered and chatting excitedly. One of the dads finally stuck two fingers in his mouth and let out an ear-piercing whistle, causing the room to fall completely silent.

"Thank you, Mr. Hamilton," Mrs. Patterson stammered. "Ladies and gentlemen, I know we're all very excited," she said crisply, holding her hands in prayer position in front of her, "but if this evening is to run smoothly, we'll all need to be paying attention.

"Guests will begin arriving shortly," she went on. "We'd like to ask the parents to go with Mrs. Cunningham to set up for the receiving line, and if the ladies and their escorts would please follow me, we'll be retiring to the back salon until the presentation. There are refreshments for you there." Totty teetered down the hall, briskly waving her hand, summoning us to follow.

Safely sequestered in the back room, Mary Katherine, Taylor, Mary Price, and I quickly staked out a corner to occupy.

"Y'all look so pretty," Taylor gushed as we sat, her eyes beginning to glisten.

"Oh God, Taylor, don't cry now! Your mascara will run," Mary Katherine scolded. "And thank you. You look pretty too," she added, at which Taylor smiled.

"My only problem," said Mary Price, trying humorously to negotiate her large skirt into the small folding chair, "is that I don't know how to sit down in this damn thing."

"Ah, the advantages of an A-line," I sighed, pulling up a chair.

Nearly an hour passed before we realized it was almost time for our grand entrance.

"Oh gosh! I better grab something to eat before we get out there, or I might faint," Taylor exclaimed, hopping up from her seat.

"Me too, if I can stuff it in here." Mary Price patted the nonexistent bulge of her belly under the white silk.

"Ya know, I better eat something, too," Mary Katherine added, winking at me as Robert approached and pulled up a seat.

"Are you guys drinking over there?" I asked, suspiciously eyeing a group of escorts huddled in the corner.

"Smalley brought a flask." I frowned disapprovingly. "But I swear I haven't had a drop!" he insisted, raising his hands defensively.

"Good."

"I don't want to be talking to your dad drunk," he laughed. "And by the way, Miss MacRae, has anyone told you you look beautiful tonight?" He grinned.

"Where'd you pick up that line?" I asked, simultaneously blushing and raising a cynical eyebrow.

Robert leaned in close, until his lips almost grazed my ear. "Smalley," he whispered.

The answer had us both cracking up, but before he pulled away, Robert planted a light kiss on my cheek. I could have melted, and had I not been surrounded by sixty of my peers at the Beaufort Country Club, about to be formally presented to society, I might have jumped him right then and there. Luckily, Mrs. Patterson, always the beacon of all things ladylike, appeared to save me from myself. Standing in the doorway, she clapped loudly, like a kindergarten teacher rounding up an unruly classroom. It was time for the presentation.

Robert and I stood. He squeezed my hand. "You ready?"

"Ready as ever." I smiled and hooked my arm through his.

TWENTY-THREE

*A lady appreciates tradition,
both her own and that of others.*

"Miss Mary Price Harding, daughter of Mr. and Mrs. Rowland Price Harding," read the announcer.

Mary Price was led by her father onto the dance floor, through two parallel lines of escorts. When she reached the front, she stopped, letting go of her father's arm, and gave a cool curtsy before stepping back to make way for the next girl.

My stomach churned. I was fourth in line. Please, *please* don't bust, I thought. Of course Gram was front row and center in the crowd that waited expectantly. *God, if you get me through this,* I bargained, *I'll start going to church* and *synagogue every week. With Gram. In a dress. And heels.*

"Miss Ann Gordon MacRae, daughter of Mr. and Mrs. Gordon Marshall MacRae, the Fourth."

Showtime. I think my father turned and smiled at me, but I can't be sure; I was floating as if in a dream. I listened to the people clapping, but didn't hear them. I looked at their smiles, but didn't see them. Every step felt like an eternity as we passed through the escorts, standing like palace guards in tuxedo tails. At the end of the line was the vast emptiness of the dance floor. I would later swear I have no memory of my curtsy (maybe I blocked it out), but apparently I made it to the front, bowed, and joined the other girls, all without tripping over myself.

Once every debutante's name had been called and all twenty curtsies had been made, the band struck up the practiced tune, and Mary Price gracefully initiated the winding figure. It was a good thing I was only asked to follow the girls in front of me, because poor Wayne's hours of impassioned instruction had completely escaped me. My mind was totally blank. I tried not to focus on faces in the crowd, afraid they'd distract me and I'd go left when everyone else went right. I only finally remembered to smile when I paired off with Taylor in the last formation. The "talent" segment over, it was time for our fathers to join us on the dance floor.

"You did beautifully," my dad whispered as we waited, poised for the music to begin again.

"I felt like a show poodle," I replied without moving my lips.

The band played the first notes of the now all-too-familiar waltz, and twenty couples stepped in perfect unison. As we danced the steps we'd rehearsed a thousand times, I felt myself finally relax, my shoulders drop, my jaw unclench.

My father held me tightly. "You look very grown-up tonight," he whispered, a hint of sadness behind his pride.

"I am grown-up, Dad. That's the point."

"Not to me."

"What are y'all gonna do without me next year?"

"*Y'all*? They've gotten to you too, huh?"

"I guess so."

"Here's the real test: what are you going to tell your college friends when they ask where you're from?"

"Ooh. Hard one." I wrinkled my nose. "Bewfud, Albama, I s'pose," I answered in my most convincing Southern drawl.

The weight of another hand fell on my shoulder. It was Robert. The escorts were cutting in for their dance. My father smiled at him and stepped aside.

"Hey," said Robert.

"Hey."

"Well done. You look like you've had some practice," he teased, as we stepped in unison. "You do this a lot, don't you? Travel to cities and pretend to be the new kid so you can make your debut all over America."

"You caught me. But the sad news is, now I have to kill you."

"Do what you have to do, but you looked great."

"Thank you, sir."

"Spoken like a true lady."

"Shut up," was my retort, but I was smiling. I couldn't stop, actually.

Robert released his hand from my waist and twirled me with his other one. I was halfway around before I remembered we weren't allowed to spin until the fourth dance. Another one of those pointless rules for rules' sake.

Anxiously, I searched the crowd. Maybe no one had seen us. Nope. Totty Patterson was shooting me a very stern look. She was not pleased. I looked away before I got a finger wag.

"Whoops," I whispered out of the side of my mouth.

"What?"

"You're not supposed to turn me till the fourth dance. House rules."

"Sorry. Must not have gotten that memo."

"Damn it, and I was doing so well!"

"It's okay."

"My grandmother's going to flip out."

"Just blame it on me."

"That's very chivalrous of you, but trust me, you don't want to be the fall guy on this one."

"She can't be that bad."

"Oh, she is," I assured.

After two more dances, with Richard and Pawpaw, I

was finally clear to mingle. When Mary Price and Mary Katherine saw me searching for them, they politely parted ways with the old people in tuxes and sparkly ball gowns congratulating them, and came to hug me.

"See, that wasn't so bad," Mary Price reassured.

"You didn't even fall!"

"Well, the night's not over yet," I hedged as Taylor came rushing up, dragging a photographer behind her.

"Let's get a picture!" she cried, clapping. It was no wild guess to say that this evening was the highlight of Taylor's life thus far. This was her element. I was happy for her.

The four of us lined up, shoulder to shoulder.

"I wish Bliss was here," I remembered sadly.

"I talked to her today. She's on a date tonight; so don't worry, she's happy." Taylor winked. "She said to take lots of pictures for her."

"Okay, ladies, say brie!" the photographer said, releasing a barrage of flashes.

"All right," I exclaimed, blinking, "there's one for the record!"

Taylor hugged me and flew off with the photographer to find her grandparents. The Marys went to refresh their drinks, and I excused myself, appropriately, to the *ladies* room. When I came out, Gram was in the hallway. Uh-oh, I thought, here it comes: the twirl reckoning.

"Hi, Gram. I'm sorry about that spin," I stammered. "I totally forgot we weren't allowed to yet. I didn't mean to . . ."

"Ann Gordon, that's enough."

I braced myself for an onslaught of indignation at my total lack of propriety. Instead, I was surprised when my grandmother's face softened. "I'm just glad you remembered to smile."

Gram must have read the look of confusion on my face, because she took me by the elbow and whispered in my ear conspiratorially, "At my ball, my mother was mortified, said I looked like a deer caught in the headlights!" Her eyes twinkled and she let out a very *un*Gramlike chuckle. "Walk with me to the coatroom. I have something I'd like to give you."

As we walked slowly down the hall, Gram stood straight and proud, but next to me, she felt small and fragile, like a wisp of the woman I remembered from my childhood. It made me sad, and I felt a tenderness bloom in me I'd never had for her before. I'd spent so much time seething over how Gram didn't understand me, I guess I hadn't put much effort into understanding her.

When we reached the coat check, Gram asked the young man behind the counter for the package she had stowed under the desk. He handed her a gift-wrapped box, and Gram directed me to a quiet corner of the room.

"I know this has not been easy for you, Ann Gordon. I'm not as insensible as you might think. So thank you for honoring an old lady's wish. I've been saving this for you," she said, handing me the present.

Carefully I opened it, trying not to rip the fancy gold-foil wrapping paper—not easy with gloves on. Inside, folded in tissue of the lightest pink, was a book, and a very old book by the look of it. The dust jacket was gone, revealing a white leather cover. The binding was cracked, and the edges were worn. On the front, embossed in gold letters was the title, *Ella May Forrester's Guide to Being a Lady.*

I looked at Gram, who was smiling, and turned it over in my hands before opening it. Each yellowing page was engraved with an old-fashioned dictum: *A lady always sends a thank-you note. A lady introduces herself in new company. A lady promptly accepts or declines an invitation. . . .* It was illustrated with line drawings of a Victorian-looking woman offering her hand to a suitor or twirling her parasol.

Gram reached over and turned to the title page. In sweeping cursive was an inscription dated July 21, 1951.

To Mary Remington Randolph,
On the day of her debut.
Beaufort, Alabama

It was signed by Evelyn Randolph—my great-grandmother. Beneath it was another inscription, with today's date. In familiar, tight script it read:

To Ann Gordon MacRae,
On the day of her debut.
Beaufort, Alabama

It was signed Mary Remington Randolph MacRae.

My eyes welled up. "Thank you, Gram," I said softly.

Finally I got it. This night was as much about Gram as it was about me. In her own way, she was creating for us a common thread.

"You're welcome, dear, but stop those tears. I won't have my granddaughter cry at her own ball." She grasped my hands, still holding the book, between her own. "Especially when she has already cried at one party." She smiled.

I laughed. "I'm fine. Thank you," I said, wiping at my eyes.

"Good. I'm going to find your father for a dance." She patted my hand and returned to the ballroom.

I handed the box back to the coat-check boy for safe keeping. Then, taking a deep breath, I smoothed my skirt and also headed back. Beside a papier-mâché oak tree, I watched the couples dance. In the midst, I caught a glimpse of my father and grandmother fox-trotting next to Pawpaw and my mother. Behind them, Mary Price danced with her father. I smiled, my heart full.

Robert appeared beside me. "Are you in trouble?"

"She decided to show mercy this time."

"Then may I have this dance, or am I on probation?"

"I think it's okay. We're safely out of the no-spin zone," I said, taking his hand and leading him to the dance floor.

He held my waist firmly, and I draped my arm over his shoulder. Who needed Clark Gable? I had my own Rhett Butler. A Rhett Butler, I might add, who had recently decided to attend a college only an hour from my own.

"So, what are you gonna tell those kids at Brown when they ask what you did this summer?"

"Hi. I'm Annie, and I'm a recovering debutante."

He laughed and spun me in a circle—twice.

acknowledgments

I owe a great big thank-you to so many people: First, to my tireless editors, Helen Perelman and Elizabeth Rudnick, who gave me all the good ideas and then let me think they were my own. Their guidance and belief in me have been the world's greatest gifts. To Roberta Pressel and Lisa Henderling, for a fabulous cover. To my patient family, who has loved and supported me in countless ways through the years, even when I am (gasp) stubborn. To my friends, especially my girls from Richmond and Sewanee. They laugh at my jokes and at me, which I love them for. I am truly blessed to call them friends. To the debs and friends who advised on early drafts, and those who offered stories, ideas, and unflagging support. A special thank-you to Erin, Meg, Ann Curran, the Southern Supper Club, and Peter Stevenson at the *New York Observer*, who all, in a roundabout way, helped this book come about. Last, but certainly not least, I offer heartfelt gratitude to Appa and Amma, through whom and in whom all things—Jai!